As you probably guessed from the picture, Atticus closely resembles me! I mean me, Henry the cat, not me, Jennifer Gray, the author. I'm thrilled to have so many fans and wanted to let you know that my, I mean, Atticus's new adventures are even funnier and more exciting than the last one. Thanks Jennifer for turning me into an action-cat hero! And thanks, you guys, for reading.

Henry (and Jennifer)

Praise for Atticus

'Atticus is the coolest cat in the world.
This is the coolest book in the world.'
Lexi, age 7

'Atticus Claw is fantastic because it has interesting
creatures and characters. I especially like Atticus.'
Charlotte, aged 8

'I think that this book is the best book I've
ever read because it's so funny!'
Yasmin, age 10

'Fun and exciting, Atticus Grammiticus
Cattypuss Claw is the most cutest. Once i
opened it i just couldn't put it down.'
Saamia, age 9

'It's mysterious – it makes you want to
read on.'
Evie, aged 7

'I would recommend it to a friend.'
Mollie, aged 10

'Once you start to read it you can't stop!'
Molly, age 8

ATTICUS CLAW
Settles a Score

Jennifer Gray is a barrister, so she knows how to spot a cat burglar when she sees one, especially when he's a large tabby with a chewed ear and a handkerchief round his neck that says Atticus Claw. Jennifer's other books include *Guinea Pigs Online*, a comedy series co-written with Amanda Swift and published by Quercus. Jennifer lives in London and Scotland with her husband and four children, and, of course, Henry, a friendly but enigmatic cat.

By the same author

ATTICUS CLAW
Breaks the Law.

JENNIFER GRAY

ATTICUS CLAW

CLAW

Settles a Score

ff

faber and faber

First published in 2013
by Faber and Faber Limited
Bloomsbury House, 74–77 Great Russell Street,
London WC1B 3DA

Printed in England by CPI Group (UK) Ltd, Croydon, CR0 4YY

A CIP record for this book
is available from the British Library

ISBN 978–0–571–28681–2

FSC
www.fsc.org
MIX
Paper from
responsible sources
FSC® C101712

2 4 6 8 10 9 7 5 3 1

To my sister
with special thanks to Henry and Dougal

Atticus Grammaticus Cattypuss Claw – formerly the world's greatest cat burglar – was feeling sick. He hated flying. Flying was for birds, not cats. In his old cat-burgling days he had always travelled by cruise ship or first-class compartment on the train rather than fly. And the hideous contraption he found himself in now was much worse than a plane. It was even worse than a helicopter or a hot-air balloon. It was tabby torture.

Atticus opened one eye then closed it again. He'd never have agreed to come on holiday to London if he'd known the Cheddar family planned to take him on *this*. He'd thought it was a giant hamster wheel when Callie first pointed it out to him. (Although he probably should have guessed that there wouldn't be too many giant hamsters roaming around London looking for exercise at the height of the tourist season.) He just wished someone had *warned* him, though. What happened to *trust*? But one minute he'd been eating a bit of Michael's fish-paste sandwich, and the next he'd been bundled up by Callie, and now here he was in a fragile-looking glass capsule dangling dangerously from the edge of a huge revolving metal circle, inching his way into the sky.

'Are you all right, Atticus?' Callie hugged him gently.

'You look a bit funny.' Michael tickled his chin. 'Do you feel sick?'

Atticus purred weakly. *Finally they'd noticed!* It was a bit late now, though. They had already lifted off.

'It's called the Eye, Atticus,' Mrs Cheddar took his paw. 'No need to worry – everyone rides it when they're visiting London. You get a fantastic view when you get to the top. Look, there's the Thames.'

The Eye? Why would anyone want to take a ride in an eye? Atticus screwed *his* eyes firmly shut. And he didn't want to see the Thames. Didn't Mrs Cheddar realise that cats *hated* water? He wanted to get off. 'Meow!' he yowled.

'Stop mollycoddling him!' Inspector Cheddar said sternly. 'He's a police cat, not a pet. He needs to toughen up.'

Atticus didn't know what mollycoddling meant but it had a nice sound to it – especially the 'cod' bit. He wondered if there were any other good fishy words humans used that he didn't know, like dolly-prawning or jolly-sardining or trolley-trouting. Right now they all sounded a lot more fun than being a police cat. His chewed ear drooped. He wondered if it was too late to change his mind.

'But we're on holiday, Dad!' Atticus felt Michael stroke his good ear.

'Thanks to Atticus,' Callie straightened the red handkerchief he wore round his neck.

'And the Tuckers,' Mrs Cheddar added.

Atticus opened one eye. The trip to London was a present from Mrs Tucker, the Cheddars' house-keeper, as a reward for Atticus

stopping being a cat burglar and starting being a police cat instead. It was Atticus who had been mainly to thank for catching Jimmy Magpie and his gang when they swooped on the Toffly Hall Antiques Fair and tried to steal Lord and Lady Toffly's tiara.

'Talking of Mr and Mrs Tucker,' Callie sighed, 'I wish they were here.'

Atticus did too. Mrs Tucker's basket was always full of freshly caught sardines off her husband's fishing boat. And Mr Tucker had loads of exciting stories about sea monsters, not to mention a fascinating beard-jumper, which was knitted together in a big tangle. All sorts of interesting morsels got stuck in it, which Mr Tucker let Atticus pick out with his claws when no one else was looking.

'I miss them too,' Mrs Cheddar said. 'But they're moving into Toffly Hall this weekend. They said we could visit them when we get back.'

Atticus's purr grew louder. He was happy for the Tuckers. The Tofflys' tiara (which they had thought was worth zillions) had turned out to be a fake, while Mrs Tucker's ruby necklace (which she had thought was a fake) had turned out to be

worth zillions. Which is why the Tuckers were moving into Toffly Hall and sending the Cheddars on holiday, and the horrible snooty Tofflys were buying an old caravan near the municipal rubbish tip and looking for work polishing spoons.

Inspector Cheddar frowned at Atticus. 'Just because you've put a few measly magpies in jail doesn't mean you can let your guard down,' he said. 'Once you're in the police force you've got to keep your eyes open twenty-four hours a day, even on holiday.'

Twenty-four hours a day! Atticus could hardly believe his ears. *Was he kidding? What about sleeping? And eating? And sitting on the sofa watching the TV? Not to mention hanging out beside the beach huts at Littleton-on-Sea with Mimi, the pretty Burmese?* That took up at least twenty-three hours a day. That left one whole hour for being a police cat! (Of course, in the old days, when he'd been a burglar, Atticus would have spent the extra hour breaking into people's houses and opening their safes with his sharp claws and stealing their jewels, but he didn't do that any more. Not since the Cheddars had given him a proper home.)

'And one other thing, Atticus,' Inspector Cheddar said, looking at Atticus's pained expression disapprovingly. 'Police cats should never be sick in public. It gives people a bad impression. Remember that if you don't want to end up on traffic cones.'

Atticus opened the other eye with a sigh. He could see the reflection of the shiny police-cat badge, which was pinned to his handkerchief, twinkling back at him from the glass of the capsule. He was very proud of his badge. And of being a police cat. He just didn't want to be one twenty-four hours a day, especially not when he was on holiday. But he didn't want to let Inspector Cheddar down either, especially as it was he who had made Atticus a police cat in the first place. He took a deep breath and jumped down from Callie's arms.

'That's better.' Inspector Cheddar began pointing out the sights. 'There's Buckingham Palace. And the Tower of London. And see that? It's Trafalgar Square. Oh and look down there. It's Big Ben!'

The children pressed their faces to the glass.

Atticus forced himself to do the same. London

unfolded beneath him. He felt his fur stiffen. It was a long time since he'd been to London, but he hadn't forgotten it. A lot of the sights looked familiar, even from this height. The view from the Eye brought back a flood of memories he thought he'd pushed away forever.

London was where he'd first learnt to be a cat burglar.

It was also where he'd had his ear chewed.

And the animal responsible for both those things made Jimmy Magpie and his gang look as innocent as poached eggs. His name was Biscuit. Ginger Biscuit. He was the world's toughest tomcat and he worked for a Russian criminal mistress of disguise called Zenia Klob. At least he used to.

They both did. Until Atticus ran away.

Suddenly Atticus forgot about hating flying. He forgot about feeling sick. He didn't feel afraid any more.

'Look at Atticus!' Michael said. 'He's feeling better.'

'He's really brave!' Callie agreed.

'Well done, Atticus,' Mrs Cheddar said.

'That's more like it.' Inspector Cheddar nodded.

Atticus hardly heard them. All he could think about was Ginger Biscuit. *Would he get a chance to put his arch-rival behind bars now that he was a police cat?* He certainly hoped so.

Almost without thinking, Atticus touched his chewed ear with one paw.

He still had a score to settle.

At about the same time that Atticus Claw was staring down on London from the Eye, three black-and-white birds with dark blue flashes to their wings and jade green feathers in their tails sat in a line on a bench in a cell in Her Majesty's High Security Prison for Bad Birds. The first was fat with a raggedy tail. The second was thinner with a hooked foot. The third, which sat slightly apart from the others, his head on one side, was a magnificent bird with glossy feathers and cruel glittering eyes. Each bird was chained to the bench by an iron ring around one foot.

With a heavy sigh the fat one got up and turned to face the wall.

'Don't!' The thin one covered his ears with his wings.

'I've got to, Slasher,' Thug retorted. 'Otherwise I'll lose count.'

~~卌卌卌卌~~ ||||

Slowly and painfully he scraped his beak along the damp brick across the last set of lines.

SSSSSCCCCCRRRRREEEEECCCCCHHHHHH!

He sat back and surveyed his work. 'Only two thousand five hundred and thirty more days to go,' he said proudly.

Slasher uncovered his ears. 'If you do that every day for the next seven years, Thug, I swear I'll mangle you.'

'It's only six years three hundred and forty days actually,' Thug told him.

'What about leap years?' Slasher demanded.

Thug looked puzzled. He started to count his claws. Suddenly he began to sob. 'I've got to get out of here!' he gurgled. 'I can't stand it any more. I think I'm losing my marbles.'

'Ah, shut up, Thug,' Slasher said, clipping him in the crop with his free foot. 'You don't *have* any marbles. It's thanks to you we're stuck here in the first place. If you'd stood up to Atticus Claw at the Toffly Hall Antiques Fair instead of surrendering as soon as he said "boo", Jimmy and me would have got away.'

'Shut your beak, Slasher,' Thug retorted, digging his cellmate painfully in the ribs with what was left of his tail. 'You weren't exactly much help from where I was hopping. You practically passed out as soon as you realised Claw was on the scene.'

'Chaka-chaka-chaka-chaka-chaka!'

'Chaka-chaka-chaka-chaka-chaka!'

The two magpies began chattering at one another angrily.

The third magpie regarded them thoughtfully with glittering eyes. 'Boys, boys, boys,' Jimmy Magpie interrupted quietly. 'Neither of you were to blame. It was *my* fault.'

Thug and Slasher gaped at him.

'But nothing's ever your fault, Boss.' Slasher squawked. 'That's what you always tell us.'

'Yeah, it's Slasher's,' Thug agreed.

'Not this time.' Jimmy shook his head impatiently. 'It was mine. I underestimated Atticus Claw. He was cleverer than I thought, especially

when he teamed up with those *humans.*' His voice dropped to a hiss.

Thug and Slasher exchanged nervous glances. It was always better to keep the conversation off humans when you were around Jimmy unless you wanted your head pecked.

'*Humans,*' Jimmy repeated to himself. 'Bird-bashing, Car-killing, Magpie-murdering *humans.*'

Thug and Slasher waited.

'CHAKA-CHAKA-CHAKA-CHAKA-CHAKA!' Suddenly Jimmy's temper snapped. He flew up into the air as far as the chain would let him and beat his wings furiously.

'I'm going to get even with Atticus Claw,' he spat, 'for getting in with those cheesy Cheddars and making me look like a brainless budgie. I'm going to peck his eyes out. I'm going to rip his whiskers off. Then I'm going to pull all his fur out and knit a nest snuggler with it.'

'I didn't know you could knit, Boss,' Thug said, impressed. 'Will you teach me?'

'I can't, you moron,' Jimmy screeched. 'It's an expression.'

Thug looked crestfallen.

'But how, Boss?' Slasher said. 'How are we gonna break out? This place is like a prison.'

'It *is* a prison, you idiot!' Jimmy Magpie squawked. 'But I've got friends on the outside. Some of the lads who got away from Toffly Hall have been putting feelers out.'

'Who?'

'Pig, Gizzard and Wally.'

Thug and Slasher grinned at one another. Pig, Gizzard and Wally were three of their favourite magpies. The five of them liked nothing better than spending a morning bullying baby birds, followed by an afternoon pooing on people's clean washing when they hung it out to dry.

'Do you remember when we all ganged up on those baby robins?' Slasher chuckled. 'And Pig told them the reason they'd got a red breast was because they'd contracted robin-rot and they all started to cry.'

'Good times!' Thug sighed.

'Apparently our little adventure at Toffly Hall got us noticed,' Jimmy landed back on the bench. 'Someone's been asking after us.'

'Some*one*?' Slasher queried.

'You don't mean . . .' Thug lowered his voice just in case . . . 'a *human*?'

'Yes, I do,' Jimmy admitted calmly. 'But not your run-of-the-mill bird-batterer. This is a human who appreciates us magpies: a human who admires our style; a human who wants to know if we'd be interested in doing a job for her.' His eyes shone. 'A human who wants *us* to help steal *her* something BIG.'

Thug's face lit up. 'What, *glittery* things?'

'Yes, Thug. Glittery things.'

'But how are we gonna get out of here?' Slasher asked again.

'Patience, Slasher,' Jimmy Magpie lay back on the bench, his wings folded behind his head. 'It's all arranged. It won't be long now: all we have to do is wait.' He closed his eyes. 'And when we've done the job, that's when we'll get even with Claw.'

Squeak . . . squeak . . . squeak . . .

The prison guard looked up from his desk. A little old lady in a shabby raincoat and a tea-cosy hat was standing in front of him, leaning on a wheelie trolley. 'Can I help you, madam?' he asked politely.

'Yes, comrade,' she said in a strange accent. 'I'm Mildred Molotov. From the Mongolian branch of Magpies Anonymous.'

'Magpies Anonymous?'

'Yes. It's a Russian charity set up to help bad birds. I need three volunteers from amongst the inmates.'

The prison guard looked puzzled. He hadn't heard of Magpies Anonymous but then he hadn't been working at Her Majesty's High Security Prison for Bad Birds for very long.

'We've got some hard cases in here, Mrs . . . er . . . Molotov,' the prison guard said doubtfully. 'Vicious villains, you might say. I'm not sure you'd want to meet them.'

'It's Ms,' the old lady snapped. 'Not Mrs. And I'm used to dealing with vicious villains.' She gave the prison guard a sugary smile. 'You could say they're my life's vork.'

'You really think it'll make a difference?' the prison guard hesitated. He believed in giving criminals another chance.

'For sure!' the old lady cried. 'Give me five min-utes with the three vorst birds you've got and I promise they von't give you any more trouble.'

'Follow me, then.' The prison guard reached for his keys. 'We'll go to Block M. Cell 13. That's where we keep the Toffly Hall gang.' He opened the first gate and set off slowly down the corridor. 'I warn you though, they're a bad bunch.'

Squeak . . . . . . squeak . . . . . . squeak.

The old lady hobbled behind him with the squeaky wheelie trolley. 'Hurry up, comrade,' she said. 'I have important vork to do.'

The prison guard quickened his pace.

Squeak . . . squeak . . . squeak.

The old lady quickened hers. 'Qvick! I haven't got all veek,' she complained.

The prison guard walked faster.

Squeak-squeak-squeak.

So did the old lady. 'Places to go, people to see,' she muttered. 'Move it!'

The prison guard broke into a run.

Squeaksqueaksqueak.

The old lady cantered alongside him.

'Here we are,' the prison guard panted. They

had arrived outside Block M. He opened the gate.

'Chaka-chaka-chaka-chaka-chaka!' The sound of chattering magpies filled the air.

'Thank you, comrade,' the old lady said. 'I'll take it from here. You can go back to your desk now.' She removed her tea-cosy hat. Her grey hair was full of sharp-looking steel hairpins.

The prison guard watched as she fiddled with one and took it out. The points gleamed in the harsh electric light. 'I'm afraid I have to come with you to the cell,' he said uncertainly. 'It's the rules.'

The old lady's face hardened. 'Vot?'

The prison guard tried a smile. 'I should really have checked your trolley too.' He bent towards it. 'It's just routine.'

'Chaka-chaka-chaka-chaka-chaka!' The magpies' chattering became even louder.

'Have a look if you like, comrade,' the old lady said softly. 'But ve don't vant you to come with us.' She shot the prison guard a venomous look. 'GET HIM, BISCUIT.'

'MMYYAAAWWWW.'

The prison guard saw a flash of ginger spring from the trolley. He felt razor-like needles catch him by the throat. He staggered backwards and toppled over.

'CHAKA-CHAKA-CHAKA-CHAKA-CHAKA!' The magpies were going mad.

The last thing the prison guard remembered was the old lady looming over him with a hairpin, and something sharp pricking his arm. Then he fell into a deep sleep.

3

At Scotland Yard the Metropolitan Police Commissioner was furious. 'You mean, she just walked into the prison as bold as brass and lifted the Toffly Hall gang? Just like that?' He threw a file down on the desk.

'Yes, Commissioner,' his deputy admitted. 'She knocked the prison guard out with a sleeping potion, probably administered by hairpin. We found one nearby. It's with Forensics.'

'How is the guard now?'

'Coming round. Keeps talking about biscuits.'

'What?' The Commissioner's eyebrows shot up.

'Yes. And something ginger jumping at him out of the trolley.'

'I see.' The Commissioner scratched his head.

'Hairpins,' he muttered. 'Biscuits.' He looked up at his deputy and swallowed hard. 'Sounds like it's Klob all right.'

'I'm afraid so, sir,' the Deputy Commissioner agreed nervously.

'That means it's going to be something BIG.'

'Looks like it, sir.'

The Police Commissioner picked up the file again. It was marked TOP SECRET. 'Who was it that caught the Toffly Hall gang?' he asked.

'Inspector Ian Cheddar,' his deputy read from some notes. 'And his highly trained police cat, Atticus Claw. According to the file he's a reformed burglar. The cat, I mean,' he added hastily, 'not Cheddar.'

'Cat?' The Commissioner gasped. 'But that's perfect!'

'It would seem so, sir,' the deputy agreed. 'Given what we're up against.'

'Can we trust him though? The cat, I mean, not Cheddar.'

'I think so, sir. Apparently the operation at Toffly Hall was brilliant: the most criminals caught in one day in the history of the force. Claw captured

the magpie ringleader and his second and third in command.'

'Hmmm, impressive. What do we know about Cheddar?'

'Recently promoted to Inspector at Littleton-on-Sea,' the deputy read from his notes. 'Previous career on traffic cones. Keen to make it up the ladder to Scotland Yard.'

'Well now's his chance.' The Police Commissioner had come to a decision. 'Get me Cheddar,' he ordered. 'And his police cat. NOW.'

An hour later Inspector Cheddar and Atticus sat opposite the Commissioner in the Commissioner's huge office at Scotland Yard.

'Sorry to drag you away from your holiday, Cheddar,' the Commissioner apologised. 'Only something's come up. We need your help.'

Inspector Cheddar couldn't believe his ears. This was his dream come true. Scotland Yard needed *his* help? Holidays didn't come any better than this. He felt like running round the Commissioner's office and jumping over the furniture: he wanted to grab the Commissioner by the ears and kiss him on both cheeks. From the look on the Commissioner's face though, he decided he'd better not.

'It's quite all right, sir,' he said, trying not to grin. 'I'm happy to be here.'

'The Toffly Hall magpie gang has escaped from prison.'

'Good.' Inspector Cheddar smirked.

The Commissioner looked at him sharply.

'I mean, good heavens!' Inspector Cheddar said quickly, sucking his cheeks in with a popping noise. 'How awful.'

'Ggrrrrrr,' Atticus growled.

'And that's not the worst of it,' the Commissioner went on. 'Our three jailbirds had help from the outside. Someone claiming to be from a Russian charity called Magpies Anonymous wormed her way into the prison guard's confidence. She got him to take her to Block M where the magpies were being held. Then she knocked him out with a hairpin laced with a sleeping potion and escaped with the prisoners.'

'Great!' Inspector Cheddar rubbed his

hands in glee. This was getting better and better. He could hardly contain his excitement.

'Are you all right, Cheddar?' the Commissioner barked. 'You don't seem to be taking this very seriously.'

'Gggrrrrr . . .' Atticus was still growling.

'I mean, great Scott, sir,' Inspector Cheddar corrected. 'It's shocking the lengths some villains will go to.'

'Quite.' The Commissioner couldn't help thinking the cat was more clued up than Inspector Cheddar. He hoped he'd made the right decision. 'Anyway, to cut a long story short, the woman we suspect of lifting the magpies is well known to the police. We think she's planning something BIG with their help. Here in London.' He pushed the file across the desk. 'Here, take a look at this.'

Atticus hopped up on to the desk and opened the file with one white paw.

The Commissioner watched him carefully. He'd heard people say that tabbies were intelligent. This one certainly seemed to be. The rest of its black-and-brown striped fur was standing on end. The picture of the wanted criminal had clearly spooked it.

Inspector Cheddar leant forward and examined the photograph.

'Is this *her*?' He couldn't keep the disappointment out of his voice. He'd been expecting an evil-looking female master criminal, not a sweet little old lady in a woolly hat and oversized raincoat. 'I hope you don't mind me saying, sir,' he added, 'she doesn't look much of a threat.'

'Oh really?' the Commissioner said. 'Well, that's not what Interpol think. They've had their best officers trying to find this woman for the last twenty years.'

'Oh.' Inspector Cheddar went red.

'Her real name is Klob. Zenia Klob. She's ex-KGB: trained by the Russians as an assassin during the Cold War. She's been giving even our most experienced MI6 agents the slip for years.' The Commissioner paused.

'An assassin?' Inspector Cheddar giggled nervously. 'Are you sure?'

'No, Cheddar, I'm making it up,' the Commissioner thundered. 'Just listen!'

'Yes, sir.'

24

'When Britain started getting friendly with the Russians she found herself out of a job so she decided to try her hand at stealing.' The Commissioner glanced at Atticus. The cat's claws were out and he was gripping the photograph with one paw, gradually shredding the edges with the other. At least *he* seemed to understand the severity of the situation.

'We think she's responsible for some of the most daring heists of the last few years,' the Commissioner said. 'Nothing is too big for her. She's rinsed every major jewellery store in every capital city in the world: she's stolen gems worth millions.'

'But how?' Inspector Cheddar was baffled. 'She looks so . . . so . . . innocent.'

'She's a mistress of disguise,' the Commissioner explained. 'She can be anything from a gypsy to a film star. She can be a dustman, a shop assistant or a security guard. She could even be me, for all you know.'

Inspector Cheddar glanced at the Commissioner. 'You do look a bit like her, sir, if you don't mind me saying so.'

'I do mind you saying so, you idiot!' the

Commissioner exploded. 'Of course she's not me. It was just an example.'

Inspector Cheddar swallowed. 'I knew that.'

'The point is, Cheddar, she's here. And she's planning something with those magpies. Your job is to find out what and stop her.'

'Yes, sir.'

'We don't have much to go on. What we do know is that hairpins laced with sleeping potion are Klob's weapon of choice – hard to detect and deadly accurate. Which makes Mildred Molotov, little old lady, one of her favourite disguises. We've just got to hope she sticks with that. Otherwise we've got no chance.' The Chief Inspector held his hand out for the file.

Atticus pushed it back to him. His fur was still standing on end.

'Obviously we don't know where she'll strike, so we've briefed all the security guards at the top jewellery stores in London to keep a look-out,' the Commissioner said. He handed Inspector Cheddar a walkie-talkie. 'They've been told to contact you IMMEDIATELY if they see anything suspicious.'

'Yes, sir.'

'And remember, Cheddar. Don't be fooled by her appearance. Use all the force you think necessary.'

'Yes, sir.' Inspector Cheddar practised a few karate chops.

'Oh, and Cheddar,' the Commissioner added. 'There's one other thing you and your police cat need to know. Klob doesn't work alone. She has an accomplice. Which is what makes you and Claw here perfect for the job.'

'How so, sir?'

'The accomplice is a cat: an evil one by all accounts. No one knows exactly what it looks like. We don't have a photo. Our only clue is in the name.'

'Which is, sir?'

'Biscuit. Ginger Biscuit.'

All of a sudden Atticus, who had been listening to the Commissioner with grave attention, gave a terrible yowl.

Back at the hotel Atticus went to lie down on the bed. He needed to think. So they *were* still around. Atticus's arch-rival: Ginger Biscuit – the world's meanest cat. And Klob too: Biscuit's owner. Not only that, but they'd sprung Jimmy Magpie and his gang out of Her Majesty's High Security Prison for Bad Birds.

Klob, Biscuit and Jimmy Magpie? No wonder the Commissioner was worried!

Atticus's mind went back to when he was a kitten. To the *squeak . . . squeak . . . squeak* of Klob's wheelie trolley. It was one of his earliest memories. He would never, ever, ever forget it in all his nine lives. He'd recognised Klob's grainy mugshot immediately. And he didn't need to see a photo of

Biscuit: Ginger's orange furry features were engraved on his brain forever. The Commissioner was right about one thing, although he couldn't know why: Atticus was perfect for the job.

Suddenly Inspector Cheddar burst into the room, the walkie-talkie glued to his ear.

'Quick!' he yelled. 'There's been a possible sighting of Klob heading towards Toffany's in Bond Street. Come on, Atticus, there's no time to lose!'

A few minutes later the taxi screeched to a halt at the bottom of Bond Street.

Inspector Cheddar jumped out, Atticus hard on his heels. 'Let's go over the plan one more time,' Inspector Cheddar panted, as they raced towards the store. 'I'll pretend I'm looking for a present for Mrs Cheddar. You stay out of sight. When I'm sure it's Klob, I'll wave these.' He drew a travel-pack of ginger nuts out of his pocket. 'When you see the signal, you take Biscuit. I'll deal with Klob. If the magpies show up we'll trap them in the revolving doors.'

Atticus didn't think it sounded like much of a

plan. But there was no time to think of a better one. Inspector Cheddar had already disappeared inside Toffany's. Atticus scampered after him just in time as the revolving door whizzed round again, nearly trapping his tail. Luckily the doorman didn't notice him as he picked his way across the floor and hid behind a large potted plant.

Atticus peered out. He found he couldn't see much except customers' feet so, one paw at a time, he climbed up the trunk of the plant and hid amongst the fronds. Gently he pushed them aside so that he could get a better view.

Toffany's was very posh. The carpet was thick, the wallpaper looked expensive, and tinkly music played in the background. Expensive jewellery twinkled beneath reinforced glass counters. It was just the sort of place Klob and Biscuit would strike.

Atticus pricked up his ears and listened carefully for a few moments, trying to catch the *squeak . . . squeak . . . squeak* of Zenia Klob's wheelie trolley. But all he could hear was the tinkly music. Klob wasn't here. And it didn't look like she was coming. They might as well go back to the hotel.

Inspector Cheddar had wandered over to a

counter in the middle of the room.

'Meow,' Atticus said softly, trying to get his attention.

Inspector Cheddar didn't seem to hear him. 'It's my wife's and my anniversary,' he said loudly to the shop assistant. 'I want the most expensive diamond ring you've got.'

'How about this one, sir?'

The shop assistant unlocked the counter and reached in. She placed a dazzling ring on a black velvet tray, put the tray on the counter and slid it towards Inspector Cheddar.

'It's lovely,' Inspector Cheddar said. 'How much is it?'

'Meow!!' Atticus tried to make himself heard over the tinkly music.

'Fifty thousand pounds, sir,' the shop assistant said.

'Your wife's very lucky!' An elderly lady with a woolly hat and long raincoat who had been standing a few feet away from Inspector Cheddar trying on watches smiled at the Inspector.

Atticus froze. Draped around her neck was a bright orange fur. *Oh no!* Suddenly Atticus realised that Inspector Cheddar didn't know what *he* knew – that when Zenia Klob and Ginger Biscuit were out burgling, Zenia always carried Ginger Biscuit in a wheelie trolley, not round her neck! He gulped. He had an awful feeling Inspector Cheddar was about to make a terrible mistake.

'Meow! Meow!! Meow!!! Meow!!!!'

Inspector Cheddar edged towards the old lady. 'I'll take it,' he said to the shop assistant. He pulled the travel pack of ginger nuts from his pocket and waved them in the air.

The signal! Atticus wriggled anxiously in the fronds.

'It must be a very special anniversary,' the old lady said.

'It is!' Inspector Cheddar looked about wildly for Atticus.

'I was married for fifty-seven years until my poor husband passed away.' The old lady got out a handkerchief and blew her nose loudly.

Inspector Cheddar waved the ginger nuts.

Atticus ignored him.

'All right then, I'll do it myself,' Inspector Cheddar muttered. He stepped in front of the old lady. 'SHUT IT, KLOB!' he yelled.

Toffany's fell silent. Everyone stared.

'I beg your pardon!' the elderly lady looked astonished.

'I said shut it, Klob, Molotov, whatever your name is! Don't think you can fool me with your pathetic disguise! And get that repulsive cat off your neck.'

Atticus cringed.

'It's a fox!' the old lady gasped, clutching the fur around her throat.

'Sure. And I'm Lady Gaga.' Inspector Cheddar grabbed the fur. He wrestled with it for a bit and then crushed it under his armpits. 'Atticus!' he grunted. 'I've got Biscuit!'

Atticus cowered in the plant. The other shoppers looked on in amazement.

'All right, Atticus,' Inspector Cheddar panted. 'Have it your way. If you won't help, I'll take Biscuit out too.' He whizzed the fox fur round by its tail and stuffed it into the open jewellery counter. 'Lock it!' he told the startled shop assistant. 'It's a vicious criminal.'

The shop assistant did as she was told.

'Now it's your turn, Klob.' Inspector Cheddar prepared to rugby-tackle the old lady.

'You're mad!' she said weakly. 'Help! Someone! Call the police! Get the Commissioner!'

One of the shoppers dialled 999 on their mobile.

'Nice try, Klob!' Inspector Cheddar wrestled the old lady to the ground. 'But I *am* the police. And the Commissioner himself told me not to take any chances with you.' He held her in an armlock.

'But I'm eighty-two!' the old lady gasped.

'Don't give me any of your sob stories!' Inspector Cheddar knelt on her back. 'Once a KGB assassin, always a KGB assassin.' He whipped out a set of handcuffs.

'I'm not a KGB assassin,' the old lady wept, 'I've got five grandchildren. I used to be a nurse.'

'Tell that to the judge,' Inspector Cheddar snarled. 'Before he throws the book at you.'

There was a shriek of sirens outside. The Commissioner raced in.

Inspector Cheddar looked up. 'I've got Klob, sir,' he panted. 'And I have to say you were right. She's one of the creepiest low-life criminals I've ever come across! Ugly too. She's got a mug that would make a mirror crack.'

'CHEDDAR!' The Commissioner's face was purple. 'WHAT ARE YOU DOING TO MY MOTHER?'

'Your . . .' Inspector Cheddar looked down at the old lady. Then he looked up at the Commissioner. Then he looked back down again. They both had the same beetley eyebrows and funny moustache. 'Oops,' he said.

Atticus covered his eyes. He peered out between his paws.

'You're off the case, Cheddar!' the Commissioner yelled. 'I'm going to recommend to your superior that you're put on traffic cones for the rest of your career! Come along, Mother.'

The Commissioner's mother hobbled out. The sirens faded away. Atticus was about to jump down from the potted plant and slope off without Inspector Cheddar noticing him when he heard a sound he recognised.

Squeak . . . squeak . . . squeak

His good ear pricked up.

Squeak . . . squeak . . . squeak.

So did his chewed one.

An old lady in a woolly hat and long raincoat came through the revolving doors, pulling a wheelie trolley. She made her way past the central counter. Atticus's green eyes widened. *Zenia Klob, a.k.a. Mildred Molotov.* It really was her this time! And she was after the ring! It was still sitting where the shop assistant had placed it, on the velvet tray on the counter. The shop assistant had forgotten to put it away.

Klob looked round quickly. Then she reached down to open the trolley. There was a flash of ginger.

Biscuit! Atticus moved faster than he ever had before, even in his cat burgling days. In a fraction of a second he had leapt on to the counter and picked the ring up in his teeth.

For an instant the two cats' eyes met.

'Claw!' Ginger Biscuit hissed.

'Biscuit!' Atticus hissed back. (Except it came out more like 'BBSSKKTT' because he was being careful not to drop the ring.)

Suddenly the shop assistant

saw Atticus. 'Thief!' she screamed.

Ginger Biscuit disappeared back into the trolley.

Squeak . . . squeak . . . squeak

Zenia Klob trundled back out through the revolving doors.

Atticus looked around helplessly. Everyone in the shop was staring at him.

'What the . . .' Inspector Cheddar had recovered himself.

Atticus's chewed ear drooped. *Now I'm for it!* he thought.

'I vasn't expecting that!'

On a barge on the Thames, Zenia Klob sat in the candle-lit cabin, eating burnt beetroot. 'I never thought I'd see Atticus again,' she said softly. 'Did you, Biscuit?'

Ginger Biscuit sat beside her dipping hairpins into a big green bottle marked SLEEPING POTION. He hissed angrily.

'I didn't think so.' Zenia stroked her evil cat lovingly, carefully avoiding the studded metal collar around his neck. Biscuit had a habit of helping himself to the sleeping potion when she wasn't looking and dipping his collar studs in it. She smiled. He really was a horrible heart-

less brute. 'It is a pity you tried to kill Atticus last time ve vere here,' she sighed. 'You vere a good team.'

'RRRRRRRRR . . .' Biscuit growled. He threw the hairpins down and retreated a little way along the sofa. Giving Zenia an evil look, he raised one paw and popped out his needle-sharp claws one by one: POP. POP. POP. POP. They sparkled in the candlelight.

'There's no need to be jealous.' Zenia held up a thick book.

SHSHSHSHHSHSHSH.

Ginger Biscuit sliced it from one end to the other. The pages fluttered to the floor.

'Atticus isn't going to bother us. He doesn't have vot it takes.' Zenia Klob put out her hand to stroke him again. 'He's not *ruthless* like you and me. Although,' she added thoughtfully, 'I vos impressed by his move today at Toffany's.' She frowned. 'I vonder vot he's up to. I thought he'd gone straight.'

'RRRRRR.' Ginger Biscuit slashed at a cushion. Bits of stuffing popped out.

Zenia Klob sighed. Biscuit was in one of his moods. 'Honestly, Biscuit, I know

you're disappointed about the diamond,' she said sternly. 'So am I. But you need to learn to control your temper.' She reached into the pocket of her huge raincoat and found a dead rat. There was a good supply of rats in the muddy banks beside the barge. Or at least there had been until Biscuit arrived. This was the last one. She'd been keeping it for emergencies. 'Look on the bright side, can't you? The police think ve're going to hit the big jewellery stores again. That's vy that brainless cop Cheddar vos at Toffany's today. They've got no idea vot ve're really after. Here!' she tossed the rat in the air.

Biscuit leapt up, his muscles bulging, and caught the rat between his teeth. CRUNCH! He gulped it down, fur and everything. The only bit he left was the stomach, which he spat out on to the table in a green wobbly mess. Sulkily, licking his lips, he crept back towards Zenia.

'That's better,' she said, stroking his tail. 'Now forget about Atticus. It's time for you to let the magpies in on the plan vile I go to the shop and buy the feather dye so I can put the finishing touches to their disguises.' She opened the hatch.

'Oh, and Biscuit,' she said. 'Don't eat them.' She grinned. 'Yet.' She disappeared.

As soon as she had gone, Ginger Biscuit jumped off the sofa and padded towards the back of the barge. He pulled open a curtain. Behind it were the sleeping quarters where the magpies were hidden. Ginger Biscuit's pale blue eyes moved over them slowly. Five of them were asleep. The other one – the leader – was playing patience with an old pack of cards. He seemed intelligent, Ginger Biscuit thought, for a bird. 'Wake them up,' he ordered. 'Zenia says it's time to tell you the plan.'

'All right.' Jimmy Magpie threw down the ace of spades.

Biscuit watched as he went round pecking the other birds on the head. When the fat one didn't wake up Jimmy gave him a good kick in the tail.

'Chaka-chaka-chaka-chaka-chaka!' the bird protested.

'Get up, Thug, or I'll let the cat pluck out all your feathers and roast you over a candle,' Jimmy said nastily.

Ginger Biscuit felt a growing respect for Jimmy Magpie: he wasn't just intelligent; he was mean too.

'Not the ginger one, Jimmy!' Thug squawked. 'There's something sinister about him. He's worse than Atticus Claw! AAARRRRHHHH!'

Ginger Biscuit pounced on him. 'Tell me what you know about Claw.'

'You tell him, Boss,' Thug gurgled. 'He's got me by the glug.'

'Claw double-crossed us,' Jimmy said. 'We hired him from Monte Carlo to steal some stuff for us in Littleton-on-Sea. Why? Is he a friend of yours?'

'AAARRRRRHHHHH!'

Ginger Biscuit's grip tightened around Thug's throat. 'He's no friend of mine,' he snarled. 'Go on.'

'Claw got friendly with the local copper and his family,' Jimmy said. 'Changed his mind about being a cat burglar. Decided he wanted to put everything back!' Jimmy's beak twisted in disgust. 'He caught us trying to steal the Tofflys' tiara. That's how we ended up in the slammer. All thanks to Claw.'

'That's what I heard.' Keeping hold of Thug, Ginger Biscuit sat back and scratched his ear with a free paw. 'So what was Claw doing in Toffany's today stealing a diamond ring?'

'You sure he was stealing it?' Jimmy asked sharply.

'Pretty sure,' Biscuit growled. 'That copper was there too. He nabbed Claw as soon as we left.'

'You mean Claw's back on burgling?' Gizzard demanded.

'No way,' Slasher gasped. 'What a crook!'

'What's Claw to you anyway?' Jimmy Magpie was watching Ginger Biscuit carefully.

'I taught him everything he knows,' Biscuit hissed. 'Except he didn't learn the most important lesson.'

'Which is?' Jimmy prompted.

'To *kill*.'

'Aaarrrrrgggghhhh!' Thug was still flapping feebly.

'We did a job in Kensington one night.' Ginger Biscuit stared into space, remembering. 'Posh house. Loads of loot. They had a parrot in a cage. I told Claw to finish it off. He didn't. The parrot

43

started squawking. Woke the whole neighbour-
hood up.' His fur rippled. 'Claw nearly got us all
caught.'

'And then?'

'Claw scarpered.'

'Leaving a bit of chewed ear behind?' Jimmy
guessed.

'Yeah.' Ginger Biscuit smirked. 'Between my
teeth.'

Thug gave a final twitch. Ginger Biscuit let go
of him.

'Is he dead?' Pig asked.

Thug didn't move.

'Looks like it,' Gizzard hopped on to Thug's
stomach and started bouncing up and down.

''Ere, let me have a go,' Wally joined in.

Ginger Biscuit flicked them off with his paw.
'He'd better not be,' he snarled. 'We need all six of
you. Alive. You!' He pointed at Slasher. 'Get the
worms.'

Slasher dug a plastic bag out from under a cushion.

'Tip 'em out.'

Gizzard, Wally and Pig fluttered over to help

Slasher. Between them they upended the bag and tipped the contents over Thug's body. Thug disappeared under a wriggling mass of squirming brown.

There was a faint sigh. Then a snort. Then a horrible sucking noise. Thug sat up, smacking his beak. His eyes were closed. There was a look of bliss on his face. 'I've died and gone to worm heaven!' he whispered.

'No, you haven't,' Jimmy gave him a smack. He turned to Biscuit. 'So what's the plan?'

The magpies watched Ginger Biscuit with beady eyes, their heads to one side.

'We're going to pull off the biggest robbery ever seen,' Ginger Biscuit told them. 'We're going to make history. We're going to have every flat-footed copper in the country foxed. We're going after the biggest, most valuable prize in the whole world.'

'The Crown Jewels?' Jimmy guessed.

Biscuit nodded. 'We're going to scoop the lot.'

'CHAKA-CHAKA-CHAKA-CHAKA-CHAKA!' The magpies all started chattering at once.

Jimmy silenced them with a look. 'With six magpies, you and Klob? How?'

45

'Call it an inside job,' Ginger Biscuit said slyly. 'That's where you guys come in. Now listen carefully and I'll tell you exactly what you have to do.'

The next morning the Cheddar family was having breakfast at the hotel. Atticus had been given a special high chair with a tray attached to it to make it easier for him to reach his food. On the tray was a dish of meaty chunks from one of the foil sachets he loved. Admittedly the tray was a bit babyish but he didn't mind too much. He liked sitting with the Cheddars around the table rather than eating from a dish off the floor. He hoped they'd buy him a chair like that when they got back to Littleton-on-Sea.

'He was trying to steal the ring, I tell you!' Inspector Cheddar pointed his fork towards the high chair.

Atticus's good ear drooped. He couldn't seem to make Inspector Cheddar understand that he hadn't been *stealing* the ring; he'd been *protecting* it from Zenia Klob and Ginger Biscuit.

'Nonsense!' Mrs Cheddar said firmly.

'Atticus wouldn't do that, Dad.' Callie scowled.

'He's not a burglar now.' Michael frowned. 'He's a police cat.'

'Not any more, he isn't,' Inspector Cheddar said. 'I'm stripping him of his badge.' He leant across the table, unpinned the badge from the red handkerchief around Atticus's neck and stuck it in his pocket.

Atticus's chewed ear drooped.

'Dad, that's a horrible thing to do!' Michael cried.

'How can you be so mean?' Callie yelled.

'Poor Atticus,' Mrs Cheddar agreed. 'You've made him upset. Look! You've put him off his food.'

Atticus didn't feel hungry any more. He stared dolefully at the meaty chunks.

'He needs cheering up,' Callie said.

'*He* needs cheering up!' Inspector

Cheddar repeated. 'What about me? I'm stuck on traffic cones for the rest of my career.'

'That's not Atticus's fault,' Michael said. 'He didn't go round attacking the Police Commissioner's mother.'

'I didn't know it was the Police Commissioner's mother!' Inspector Cheddar shouted. 'I thought it was Zenia Klob.'

'Atticus must have realised it wasn't her,' Mrs Cheddar said. 'That's why he didn't go after the fox fur.'

'He didn't go after the fox fur because he was too busy going after the ring!' Inspector Cheddar retorted.

Atticus gave a strangled meow.

'No,' Mrs Cheddar was watching Atticus closely. 'I really don't think he'd do that. You knew it wasn't Klob, didn't you, Atticus?'

Atticus felt his appetite returning. At least somebody understood him. His throat began to rumble.

'Listen, Mum,' Michael said. 'He's purring! You must be right.'

'So let's think.' Mrs Cheddar gave Atticus a bit of crispy bacon off her plate. 'How would Atticus know it wasn't Zenia Klob?'

'What about the photo the Commissioner showed him?' Michael asked.

'It was a rotten photo,' Inspector Cheddar said crossly. 'It could have been any old biddy. I'm telling you it looked exactly like the Police Commissioner's mother.'

'Hmmm. Not the photo then,' Mrs Cheddar gave Atticus a bit of sausage. 'So how?'

Atticus made another strangled yowl.

'Maybe he's seen Zenia Klob before,' Callie suggested.

Atticus's ears pricked up.

'Maybe he knows who she really is,' Michael said.

Atticus's whiskers twitched.

The children turned to one another excitedly. They were thinking the same thing.

Zenia Klob was a burglar. Atticus used to be one too. 'Maybe Atticus used to work for Zenia Klob!' they said at the same time.

Atticus was purring like a tractor. *Bingo!*

'Rubbish!' Inspector Cheddar wiped his mouth with his napkin. 'Zenia Klob is a world-famous criminal mistress of disguise. Atticus is a tubby tabby who just happens to have a habit of nicking shiny things when he gets the chance. Like those mangy magpies.'

'But, Dad . . .' the children protested.

Mrs Cheddar put her finger to her lips to silence them. She winked at Atticus. 'Let's talk about it later,' she said.

Atticus purred throatily. She knew they were right!

Inspector Cheddar stood up. 'What are we doing today?'

'We're going to the Tower of London,' Mrs Cheddar said. 'Come on, Atticus.' She released the tray and picked him up. 'We're going to see the Crown Jewels.'

Atticus had heard about the Crown Jewels, but he'd never actually seen them. He felt excited as Michael carried him off the Tube and they walked out from the dark Underground station into the sunshine. He stared. The Tower of London stood before him. Atticus had never seen anything like it before. It was enormous! Thick stone walls peppered with round towers rose up into the sky. A huge empty moat ran around the edge. In the middle stood a gigantic square building with four high turrets.

'Arrowholes!' Michael said. The towers were spotted with tiny black windows.

'That's the White Tower in the middle,' Mrs Cheddar consulted her guidebook. 'It says here it's where they used to torture people.'

'Let's go and have a proper look!' Michael put Atticus down. 'I'll bet there are some good ghost stories too.'

They set off around the moat to buy tickets. Just beyond the ticket office Atticus noticed a row of old shops.

TOWER VAULTS

He sniffed. He could smell fish and chips. He hoped they'd go there later.

'Come on!' Mrs Cheddar led the way to the entrance to the Tower.

'Who are *they*?' Callie stopped and stared. Two men in knee-length blue and red coats with matching hats stood beside the drawbridge.

'They're called beefeaters,' Michael said. 'We learned about them at school.'

Beefeaters! Atticus's ears pricked up. It was another interesting human word he didn't know. He wondered if a cat could be a beefeater. He liked beef. He thought he might volunteer.

'They used to guard the prisoners at the Tower,' Mrs Cheddar read from her book. 'And now they look after the Crown Jewels and show tourists round. It says here they're all ex-soldiers.'

Inspector Cheddar gave Atticus a look. 'So don't think you can get away with stealing anything else,' he muttered.

'What do you want to see first?' Mrs Cheddar asked. 'The ravens or the Crown Jewels?'

Ravens? Atticus was puzzled.

So was Callie. 'Ravens?' she repeated. 'Why do they keep ravens at the Tower of London?'

One of the beefeaters stepped forward. 'There's a legend here at the Tower,' he said in a loud whisper. 'If the ravens ever leave, the White Tower will fall. And if the White Tower falls, the monarchy goes with it.'

'What, you mean we wouldn't have a queen any more?' Michael gasped.

'Exactly.' The beefeater was eyeing Atticus. 'If the ravens leave, it's curtains for Her Majesty and the rest of the royal family. Zip. Finished. Bye-bye.'

'What a lot of twaddle!' Inspector Cheddar guffawed.

The beefeater glared at him. 'Her Majesty doesn't think so. Which is why we keep our ravens under the close eye of Her Majesty's Raven Master.' He coughed. 'Ron to his friends.'

'Can we see them?' Callie asked.

'*You* can.' The beefeater was still eyeing Atticus. 'But I'd rather you didn't take your cat,' he said, 'for obvious reasons.'

'Atticus won't eat them,' Michael said. 'He's just had breakfast.'

'Hmmm.' The beefeater didn't look convinced. 'Well, all right then, but keep him well away from our birds if you don't want him executed for treason.'

Atticus gulped. He didn't like the sound of that.

The Cheddars walked along the bridge and under the portcullis into a cobbled street. 'This is where all the shops used to be,' Mrs Cheddar read from her book. 'They used to bring in supplies along the Thames.'

There was a heavy iron door to their right. Inspector Cheddar peered through the grate. 'Come and have a look, kids. The river's just here. There are some steps down.'

'Oh yeah!' Michael stood on tiptoe. 'Here, Atticus, do you want to see?'

Atticus felt himself being picked up. He put an eye to the grate. The tide was out and the slimy steps led down to a muddy bank. Resting on top of the muddy bank was an old barge. It looked like a houseboat, although not a very well kept one. Grimy curtains were pulled across the windows and there were dead potted plants on the deck. Atticus shivered. He'd hate to live somewhere like that. It was probably full of rats. He meowed to get down.

'I think it's this way to the ravens,' Mrs Cheddar moved off towards an archway on the left. 'Come on.' The others followed.

Atticus crept along behind them. The height of the walls made him feel very small. On the other side of the archway he glanced at a signpost that pointed up some steps.

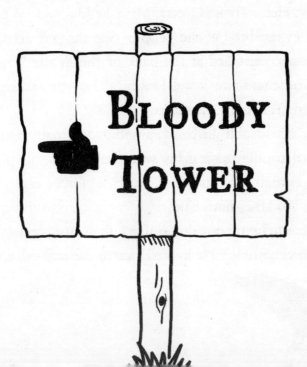

Atticus flinched. What a horrible name! This place was giving him the creeps.

'Come on, Atticus, hurry up!' Michael called.

Atticus scampered after the children. He didn't want to get left behind.

'There they are.' Mrs Cheddar peered through a grille in an ancient wall opposite the steps.

The ravens were sunning themselves in large wire pens on the lawn in front of the White Tower. Next to the pens was a wooden hut.

'This way.' Mrs Cheddar led off again.

Atticus charged after her. He wondered how long it was until lunch time.

'That's Tower Green,' Mrs Cheddar said. 'Where they used to behead people.' She shot off across a huge courtyard at the back of the White Tower. 'And that's the Jewel House.' They turned right. 'And that's the Museum.'

Atticus felt his head spinning. Normally he had no trouble finding his way round, but this place was really confusing!

'And the that's café!'

Atticus meowed. Couldn't they just stop for a quick sardine?? He looked hard at the café entrance.

'And here we are!' Mrs Cheddar doubled back across the lawn.

'Hurry up, Atticus,' Inspector Cheddar told him crossly.

Atticus decided he hated sightseeing.

'They're ugly!' Callie whispered, when they finally arrived at the raven pens. She stared at the grumpy-looking black birds. 'Waarrrk!' one of them said.

'They're like the magpies,' Michael pulled a face. 'Only bigger.'

'They're from the same bird family.' A large beefeater with a red nose appeared from inside the hut carrying a mug of tea with RON written across it. 'Corvus, it's called. It includes crows, rooks, jackdaws, jays, magpies and ravens.'

Atticus bared his teeth. He hated crows and magpies. He didn't know much about rooks, jackdaws and jays, but from where he was standing, ravens didn't look much better.

'All of them are highly intelligent,' the Raven Master said. 'They're thought to be amongst the cleverest species of animal in the world, apart from humans, obviously.'

'*And cats,*' Atticus growled, although of course nobody understood him.

'We know how clever magpies are,' Callie said.

'We caught the Toffly Hall gang,' Michael explained proudly.

'Ah, that was you, was it? I thought I recognised your cat.' The Raven Master squinted at Atticus. 'I read about the Toffly Hall arrests in the paper.' He chuckled, gesturing towards the ravens. 'I told my birds about it. They seemed quite pleased. They kept running up and down squawking. I don't think they like magpies very much.'

At least that's something we agree about! Atticus thought.

'Would you like to see me feed them?' The Raven Master went back into the hut and re-emerged with a large bowl. He held it under their noses.

'EEUUUGHHH,' Callie pulled a face.

'Chopped meat and bird biscuits soaked in blood,' the Raven Master said cheerfully. 'They get six ounces each a day. Then once a week they get an egg and a rabbit. Ravens go mad for rabbit. They enjoy ripping up the fur.'

'That's revolting,' Inspector Cheddar said.

The Raven Master shrugged. 'Not if you're a raven.'

Callie counted the fluttering birds. 'Why are there six?' she asked.

'Six is the magic number,' the Raven Master explained. 'Any less than that and the monarchy falls. Normally we keep a few extra just in case, but they're having their bird-flu jabs this week and the vet came this morning to take the others away. She's doing them in batches so we always have six here.'

'Do you ever let them out?' Michael asked.

'We do most days,' the Raven Master told him. 'They can't fly far because their wings are clipped. But like I said, this week they're confined to barracks so the vet can catch them.'

'Do you believe in the legend?' Mrs Cheddar asked. 'Do you think the monarchy will fall if the ravens leave the Tower?'

'Of course I do!' the Raven Master stood up straight and saluted. 'My job is probably the most important one in the whole country, especially this week. If any of these ravens were to disappear that would be the end of Her Majesty.'

'The other beefeater was worried Atticus might eat them,' Callie said.

Atticus swallowed. Eat *them*? No thanks.

'I don't rate his chances,' the Raven Master chortled. 'I don't think he'd be able to. They're a bloodthirsty lot, my birds. I reckon they'd have *him* for dinner not the other way round. They probably think *he's* a big, juicy rabbit.'

Atticus backed away. He didn't like the way the Raven Master was looking at him.

'Waaarrrkk!'

Or the ravens for that matter.

'Talking of food,' the Raven Master added, 'It's my lunch time.' He opened the door to the hut and stepped inside. 'Come back later though,' he winked at the children, 'and I'll tell you some ghost stories.'

'There's no such thing as ghosts,' Inspector Cheddar snorted.

Ron raised his eyebrows. 'I'd like to hear you say that if you were here on your own after dark!' He shut the door.

Atticus and the Cheddars trooped

off across the grass in the direction of the café. Atticus was exhausted. He longed for one of the hotel's nice comfy beds.

'You wait out here with Atticus,' Mrs Cheddar told her husband. 'We'll go and get some sandwiches.' She disappeared inside the café with Michael and Callie.

Atticus flopped on to a bench. It was warm in the sun. He felt sleepy.

Inspector Cheddar picked up the guidebook and started to read.

Squeak . . . squeak . . . squeak.

It couldn't be! Atticus's ears twitched. He shook his head. *No!* He must be hearing things.

Squeak . . . squeak . . . squeak.

There it was again! Suddenly Atticus felt wide awake. He wasn't hearing things! It was the squeaky wheelie trolley. Zenia Klob and Ginger Biscuit were here.

He looked around anxiously. *Squeak . . . squeak . . . squeak.*

Wait! There she was!

A woman in a green cotton tunic and matching trousers was making her way slowly across the lawn towards the ravens. The squeaky wheelie trolley trailed behind her. It was Klob!

Atticus leapt off the chair.

'Where are *you* going?' Inspector Cheddar shouted.

Atticus ignored him. He started to weave his way between the tourists.

'Come back!' Inspector Cheddar was on his feet.

Squeak . . . squeak . . . squeak.

Atticus dodged across the grass.

'I said, come back!' Inspector Cheddar dodged after him.

Atticus had a clear view of Klob now. She was only a few paces away. He braced his strong hind legs and sprang. *SHWUMP!* He landed on top of the trolley. The trolley lurched under his weight.

'Chaka-chaka-chaka-chaka-chaka!'

'HSSSSSSSSSSSS!'

Atticus gripped the trolley. The magpies were in there. With Ginger Biscuit.

64

Zenia Klob rounded on him, her eyes wide with surprise. 'You again!' She let go of the trolley and reached under her wig.

Atticus swallowed. She was going for a hairpin! There was only one thing he could do. Screwing up his courage, he fluffed out his fur and prepared to leap at her.

'Get off!' Inspector Cheddar had reached the scene. He grabbed Atticus firmly round the tummy.

'Meow!' Atticus howled.

'I'm terribly sorry,' Inspector Cheddar apologised. 'About my cat.'

Zenia Klob patted her wig. 'Don't vorry,' she said, her eyes on Atticus. 'I'm a vet: I'm used to animals. I expect he just vanted to say hello, didn't you, kitty.' She put out a hand to stroke him.

A vet! That was a new disguise. Atticus shied away from the gnarled fingers. He scrabbled to get free. The hand kept coming towards him. Atticus stuck out his claws and lashed at it.

'Atticus!' Inspector Cheddar shouted. He tucked him under his arm in a vice-like grip. 'He's not normally like this,' he said.

Zenia Klob blinked at Atticus. 'Maybe you should think about having him put down?" she suggested. 'I could do it now if you like.'

Atticus hissed and spat.

'Is everything all right?' Mrs Cheddar ran up with Callie and Michael.

'Atticus just attacked the vet!' Inspector Cheddar wrestled with Atticus.

'Oh no!' Mrs Cheddar exclaimed. A drop of blood oozed from the scratch. 'Here! I have a tissue in my bag.' She offered it to the vet.

'You should get his claws removed,' Zenia Klob said coldly, wiping her hand on the tissue. 'Vun by vun. I'd do it myself only I have an appointment vith the beetrooteater who looks after the ravens. Maybe another time?' With a last furious glare at Atticus she reached for the trolley handle and walked off.

Inspector Cheddar dangled Atticus in front of him. 'You're in big trouble, pussycat,' he said grimly.

Atticus's chewed ear drooped.

'You're grounded for the rest of the holiday.'

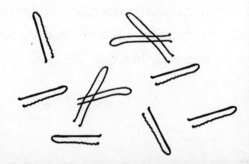

8

'I wonder what made Atticus behave like that.' Mrs Cheddar watched Inspector Cheddar lump Atticus away towards the exit. Atticus was still struggling to get free.

Callie frowned. 'He didn't like that vet.'

'She wanted to pull Atticus's claws out,' Michael shivered.

'Vun by vun,' Callie said, mimicking her.

'Wait a minute!' Mrs Cheddar cried. 'Isn't Zenia Klob a mistress of disguise?'

Michael and Cally stared at her.

'You're right, Mum!' Michael said. 'And that vet had a Russian accent!'

'She called the beefeater a beetrooteater!' Callie gasped.

'It's got to be her,' Mrs Cheddar exclaimed. 'Besides, Ron said the vet's already been this morning. So Atticus *can* recognise her, just like you two said.'

'Look, there she is!' Michael hissed.

Zenia Klob was approaching Ron's hut. There was no one else beside the raven pens. Most of the tourists were either queuing for the White Tower or having lunch in the café. She parked her trolley beside the pens, looked around to make sure she wasn't being followed, then let herself in to the hut.

'What's she up to?' Mrs Cheddar muttered.

After a moment Zenia Klob reappeared, closing the door behind her. She laid the trolley on the ground and squatted down beside the raven pens. The ravens fluttered towards her.

The Cheddars heard a faint clang.

Callie's eyes were round. 'You don't think she's going to steal them, do you?'

'I can't see!' Mrs Cheddar hissed. Klob's body was blocking her view. 'No, wait. They're still there, thank goodness.' A flutter of black birds hopped about in the pens.

Suddenly there was a flash of ginger. 'Biscuit!' Mrs Cheddar breathed.

'No wonder Atticus went nutty!' Callie said.

'She's leaving,' Michael whispered.

Zenia Klob stood up and grabbed the trolley handle. She cut left and disappeared down some steps.

Squeak . . . squeak . . . squeak.

The sound of the trolley faded into the distance.

'Quick! See if the ravens are all there,' Mrs Cheddar raced over with the children. 'I'll check Ron.'

Carefully Callie and Michael inspected the pens. The ravens were hopping about excitedly. *One . . . two . . . three . . . four . . . five . . . six.* They counted them a few times just to be sure.

'They're all here, Mum,' Callie shouted. 'Don't worry.'

One of the ravens looked at the children slyly. 'Whaka-whaka-whaka-whaka-whaka!' it chattered.

Another one with glittering eyes pecked it viciously.

'Waark!' the other ravens cried. 'Waark!'

69

Michael frowned. Was it his imagination or were the ravens behaving strangely?

'Ron's out cold!' Mrs Cheddar called from the hut.

Michael forgot about the ravens and ran to the hut with Callie. They stopped dead. Ron the Raven Master was lying on the floor of the hut in a pool of cold tea. He was sound asleep.

'I'll go and get help. You two stay here. If Klob reappears, run!' Mrs Cheddar galloped off. In a few minutes she returned with some more beefeaters and the Tower doctor.

'Will he be all right?' Michael asked. The Raven Master started to snore.

The Tower doctor took out his stethoscope and examined the Raven Master carefully. 'He'll be fine once he's slept off the effects of the sleeping potion,' he said.

'Sleeping potion?' Michael exclaimed.

The doctor nodded. 'A fast-acting knock-out drug administered by this.' He picked up a V-shaped piece of thin metal off the floor with a pair of tweezers.

'A hairpin!' Mrs Cheddar gasped.

'Jabbed into his neck just here.' The doctor pointed

to two specks of blood just below Ron's jowls.

'Like the prison guard,' Michael remembered. 'So we were right. It really *was* Klob.'

'Who's Klob?' the doctor demanded.

'A criminal mistress of disguise,' Michael explained.

'She's ex-KGB,' Callie added.

The doctor's eyebrows shot up. 'Sounds like a nasty piece of work,' he said. 'What was she doing here, apart from flattening Ron?'

'I don't know.' Mrs Cheddar looked worried. 'But we'd better get back to the hotel. My husband's the police officer in charge of catching her. At least he *was*. We need to tell him what happened.'

Two hours later, the doctor was still sitting in the hut twiddling his stethoscope.

Some policemen had taken away the hairpin in a plastic bag. An ambulance crew had removed Ron the Raven Master on a stretcher. The beefeaters had gone back to showing visitors around. And here *he* was, still stuck guarding ravens.

He wished Ron would wake up and get back to

work. The doctor had other jobs to do besides sitting around playing nanny to birds. And he was fed up with kids barging into the hut and asking him to tell them ghoulish stories about the Tower. Apparently Ron was famous for it. He had a little book full of ghostly goings-on tucked away in a drawer, which the doctor had to read so that *he* could tell the stories instead.

Why was it, the doctor wondered, that kids were so fascinated with gore? They especially loved the tale about the bloke who'd had his head sewn back on after it had been chopped off so the family could have his portrait painted. Anne Boleyn's headless ghost was popular too, as was the weeping of the wailing woman, the chink-chink of the polar bear's chains and the heavy tread of the axe man's footsteps.

The doctor didn't believe in ghosts. He didn't believe in the gory stories. And he didn't believe the legend about the monarchy falling if the ravens left the Tower. On the other hand, he didn't want to be the one responsible for letting it happen if it was true. The beefeaters would get mad. And they carried pikes – great long sticks with a sharp point on the end. In the old days they'd have used the pike to run a traitor through. By the look of some of them, he thought they still might.

The doctor sighed. Like it or not, he was stuck here for the moment. He wandered out to take a look at the birds. The doctor squatted down by the pens and pulled a face. The ravens looked like a lot of ruffians to him. There was one with a hooked foot, another that chattered instead of croaked, and three ugly-looking beasts, one of which had a nasty habit of pooing in its water. Only one of the birds looked intelligent. It had bright glittering eyes and a way of putting its head to one side as if it understood you. The doctor wondered if it knew what an important job it had – stopping the monarchy from falling. Then he laughed at himself. Birds didn't know things like that. Even if it *was* true.

The doctor went back inside the hut and banged the door shut.

Squeak . . . squeak . . . squeak.

There was a knock at the door. He looked up. It

was nearly closing time. He didn't want any more visitors. He'd had enough for one afternoon. If one more snotty kid came and asked him about whether people still blinked after they'd been beheaded he'd scream.

'Go away!'

But it wasn't a kid's head that appeared round the door of the hut. It was an old, tough-looking, bloodless sort of woman's head with wiry grey hair. The doctor found himself imagining it rolling off a wooden block and plopping on to the grass. He rubbed his eyes. Really, he thought, he needed to go home!

'We're closed,' he said.

'Not for me, you're not,' the woman said. She opened the door and stepped in, pulling a wheelie trolley behind her with a vicious-looking pike sticking out of it.

'Who are you?' the doctor blinked.

'I'm Griselda Grump, the temporary Raven Mistress.' The woman was wearing the blue and scarlet uniform of the beefeaters. Beneath the knickerbockers she wore a pair of big heavy boots. She pulled a hat out of the trolley and shoved it on.

The doctor thought he saw a flash of ginger. He shook his head. He was so tired he was seeing things. 'Boy, am I glad to see you, Miss Grump,' he said jovially. 'I thought I was going to be stuck with these rotten ravens forever.'

'It's Ms, not Miss!' the woman shouted. 'And how dare you call them rotten, you measly maggot? These birds are the property of Her Majesty, the Queen. More loose talk like that and I'll report you as a traitor and have you arrested.' She eyed him nastily. 'I might even pike you myself.'

'All right, keep your head on,' the doctor retorted. (He meant to say 'hair' but he still couldn't get the axe man out of his brain.) 'How's Ron?'

'Tired,' the woman answered shortly. 'He von't be back for a vhile.'

'Any news on the police hunt for Klob?' the doctor put his stethoscope in his bag and closed it. 'I'm just wondering if you'll be okay if she comes back.' He picked up the bag.

'Klob doesn't bother me,' the woman cracked her knuckles. 'I'm more than a match for her.'

The doctor could believe it. This one looked like an ex-sergeant major.

'Well, have fun, then.' He stepped out of the hut and closed the door behind him. His footsteps faded away.

'Oh, ve vill,' Griselda Grump chuckled. 'Lots and lots of fun. Von't ve, Ginger?'

From the depths of the trolley came a savage 'MYYYAWW.'

'Out you come, then.'

Ginger Biscuit climbed out of the trolley and jumped down.

'Shall I get the keys?' Zenia Klob asked him. 'Or vill you get those mangy magpies out yourself?'

POP. POP. POP. POP. One by one Biscuit popped out his claws.

'Vait! I'll check the coast is clear.' Zenia stuck her head out of the hut. The last of the tourists were filing out of the Tower. No one was around. 'Okay.'

Biscuit sauntered over to the raven pens and fiddled with the lock.

PING! The lock sprang open.

'Chaka-chaka-chaka-chaka-chaka!'

The magpies chattered and hopped.

'Be quiet!' Zenia Klob reached into her trolley. 'Ve need to get the equipment ready. It's nearly time to start the broadcast.'

9

'I'm baffled,' the Commissioner said.

'So am I,' the Deputy Commissioner agreed.

Atticus sat on the desk in the Commissioner's office, listening to the conversation. Now that everyone knew he could recognise Zenia Klob, he and Inspector Cheddar were back on the case. Atticus just hoped it wasn't too late.

'What do you make of it, Cheddar?' the Police Commissioner scratched his head. 'Why would Klob go into the hut disguised as a vet and knock the Raven Master out?'

Atticus was puzzled about that too. It didn't make any sense.

'I have no idea,' Inspector Cheddar shrugged. 'Unless she was after his keys.'

'He only had keys to where the ravens are kept,' the Deputy Commissioner said, 'And she didn't take them.'

'I thought she was going to steal the ravens,' Callie spoke up. 'Didn't I, Mum?'

'Yes,' Mrs Cheddar frowned, 'you did.'

'That's very clever of you, young lady,' the Commissioner sounded impressed. 'Er . . . why would she do that, though?'

'I don't know,' Callie admitted.

'The obvious target is the Crown Jewels,' Mrs Cheddar said. 'Maybe Zenia Klob thought if she stole the ravens, she could hold the Queen to ransom and demand that she hand them over. Otherwise the monarchy would fall.'

'Yes, but she'd have to keep the ravens there,' Michael said. 'Or the monarchy would fall anyway and she wouldn't get paid. She'd have to hide them somewhere at the Tower.'

'I can see where you're coming from young man but the fact is she *didn't* steal them,' the Deputy Commissioner sighed. 'They were all accounted for. Six ravens. All present and correct. You said so yourself.'

'That's true,' Michael agreed. 'Although there was something odd about them.'

'Odd?' the Commissioner repeated.

One of them made a different noise.'

'I think you must be imagining things,' the Commissioner said, not unkindly. 'Ravens are ravens, and remember, you'd only seen them once before.'

'What about the others?' Mrs Cheddar asked. 'The ones that went for their bird-flu jabs?'

'They're accounted for,' the Commissioner said. 'We contacted the real vet. She was planning to return them tomorrow and pick up some more.'

Atticus picked at his claws. The obvious target for Klob was the Crown Jewels. What could she want with the Raven Master? And what was with the vet disguise?

Just then, a junior police officer rushed in. 'I'm sorry to disturb you, sir,' he said, his face purple, 'but I think you'd better turn on the TV.'

'The TV?' the Commissioner repeated furiously. 'We're in the middle of an important meeting.'

'I'm sorry, sir, but this is an emergency.' The junior police officer strode towards a screen on the wall opposite the Commissioner's desk, grabbed the clicker from the shelf below and switched it on. 'It's Klob, sir. She's making a broadcast. She's jammed all the other channels.'

'Klob?' The Police Commissioner's mouth fell open.

The Cheddars turned round and gazed at the screen. So did Atticus.

A picture of Zenia Klob wearing a beefeater uniform and heavy army boots appeared. In the background was the Raven Master's hut.

'This is Griselda Grump, beetrooteater, also known as Zenia Klob, mistress of disguise, broadcasting to you from the raven pens at the Tower of London,' she said.

Atticus growled.

'I have a message for Her Majesty the Queen.' She grinned at the camera. 'And I'd advise you to listen up, Queenie, if you know vot's good for you.'

'Somebody arrest her!' the Police Commissioner shouted. 'Get hold of the other beefeaters now! This is treason!'

Zenia Klob narrowed her eyes. She poked a

finger at the camera. 'And before you think about getting those bumbling beetrooteaters to arrest me, you'd better hear me out if you still vant to be on the throne tomorrow.'

The camera panned in on Zenia Klob's ugly mug. Atticus shivered. She hadn't changed a bit: the same cruel eyes and thin mean mouth he remembered from when he was a kitten.

'Perhaps we'd better listen to what she's got to say, sir,' the Deputy Commissioner said nervously.

The Commissioner poured himself a glass of water. He was sweating.

'Earlier today I vent to the raven pens cunningly disguised as a vet vith my brilliant accomplice and camera-cat, Ginger Biscuit,' – a paw waved in front of the camera – 'zapped the Raven Master and svitched the ravens for different birds. I knew, of course, that there vould only be six ravens present at that time as the others vere avay for their bird-flu jabs.'

Everyone gasped. 'So that's what she was up to!' Mrs Cheddar whispered.

Atticus stared hard at Inspector Cheddar. If only *he'd* believed it when Atticus tried to tell him the vet was Klob, they could have stopped her. Inspector Cheddar seemed to be thinking the same thing. He gave Atticus a weak grin.

'In their place,' Zenia Klob continued, 'I substituted the Toffly Hall magpie gang who I lifted from Your Majesty's High Security Prison for Bad Birds only two days ago, along with three of their magpie mates.'

The magpies! Atticus stared at the screen. *Of course!* He'd heard the magpies chattering in the trolley when he leapt on it. He should have realised what Zenia had in mind.

But they didn't look anything like magpies!' Mrs Cheddar protested.

Zenia Klob was looking pleased with herself. 'Those raven suits I made for them vorked a treat!' she boasted.

'She's bluffing!' the Commissioner banged his fist on the desk.

'And if you think I'm bluffing, vatch this.'

The camera shifted to the raven pens. The wire doors hung open. Lined up outside the pens were six birds. Atticus felt his fur prickle. One had a hooked foot. A second chattered loudly. A third had glittering black eyes. Atticus didn't know the other three but the Toffly Hall gang could be disguised as chickens and he'd still recognise them anywhere. Slasher, Thug and Jimmy Magpie: looking as cocky as ever. He began to hiss.

Zenia Klob reached down, grabbed Thug and held him upside down by his feet.

'Chaka-chaka-chaka-chaka-chaka!'

'Shut up!' Zenia shouted. 'Pass me the dye-stripper, Ginger.'

The camera wobbled a bit, then the paw appeared again clutching a dark green bottle.

'I said the dye-stripper, Ginger, not the sleeping potion,' Zenia said fondly. 'You and your little tricks, you naughty boy!'

'Chaka-chaka-chaka-chaka-chack!' Thug flapped his raven wings furiously.

'Hold still, birdie,' Zenia took a second bottle from the outstretched paw. 'Or I'll let Ginger do it.'

Thug froze.

'That's better.' Zenia peeled the raven suit off Thug with her teeth. Then she tipped the contents of the bottle over him to remove the remnants of the feather dye and gave him a good shake. Black droplets scattered over the grass. 'See?' She held him up to the camera. 'A magpie.' She dropped Thug on the floor and gestured to the rest. 'So instead of your six precious ravens, Queenie, vot ve have here is half a dozen thieving magpies.'

'Chaka-chaka-chaka-chaka-chaka!'

Zenia Klob dropped the empty bottle on the grass. Atticus caught a glimpse of the label.

THUMPERS'

Traditional Dye-Stripper
For All Your Colour Removal Needs

Thumpers' traditional? Mr Tucker used Thumpers'
Traditional to dye his beard-jumper white. Atticus
wondered where the shop was. Zenia must have
gone there to get supplies since she arrived in
London.

'But don't vorry, ma'am,' Zenia sniggered.
'Ve've hidden them here in the Tower. That's vy
you're still at Buckingham Palace and haven't been
slung out into the street yet by a revolting rabble.'
She chuckled at the thought.

'We've got to find those ravens!' the
Commissioner pounded the desk with his fist.

'And forget about finding the ravens,' Zenia
Klob snarled. 'They're in a place no human vill
ever discover. Ginger is taking good care of them,
aren't you, my pet?' The paw waved in front of the
camera. Zenia glared into the lens. 'They're safe.
And so are you, Queenie. For now. Although . . .'
she added slyly . . . 'I'd vatch it, if I vere you. Ginger
has a huge appetite.' POP. POP. POP. POP. The
paw waved again, this time with four needle-sharp
claws curving from the end of it.

Inspector Cheddar gulped.

The Commissioner shook with fear.

The Deputy Commissioner passed out.

Mrs Cheddar and the kids huddled together.

Atticus flattened his ears.

'So this is vot's going to happen. Ve'll leave the ravens somevere you can find them at the Tower only if you agree to our demands. Then you get to keep the throne and ve get to run off with the Crown Jewels. It's quite simple really.' Zenia produced a list from her pocket and read it out.

DEMANDS

One. Evacuate the Tower.

Two. Disarm the security system.

Three. Have a cargo plane ready for me to fly out of City Airport to my beloved home of Siberia vith the Crown Jewels.

Four. Or else.

'If you don't do as ve say,' Zenia Klob stamped her boots, 'Ginger vill kill the ravens. Vot he doesn't eat he'll chuck in the Thames. And you can vave bye-bye to your throne, lady. Britain, like my own vonderful country – Russia – will become a Republic. You have until dawn.'

The screen started fizzing. It went fuzzy, then black.

There was silence for a few moments.

BRRIINNNNGGGG! The sound of the ringing phone startled everyone.

The Commissioner picked it up. He clicked the button for loudspeaker. 'Yes, what is it?' he demanded.

'I have the Queen on line one, sir,' the operator said. 'She wants to see you at the Palace. At once.'

Two panda cars were waiting for them at the entrance to Scotland Yard. The drivers held the doors open. Inspector Cheddar and the two senior policemen jumped into the first one. Atticus, Mrs Cheddar and the children scrambled into the second.

'Belt up!' the driver ordered. 'Including the cat.'

Atticus was on the back seat, in the middle between the two children. Michael pulled the belt across him. *Click*! His head poked out between the two straps. 'We're ready!' Michael said.

NEE-NAW. NEE-NAW. NEE-NAW.

The panda car sped away. It whizzed along the street, overtaking cars and buses. Pedestrians stood on the pavements gawping.

'Hold on,' the driver said, swerving on to the

wrong side of the road to get past a lorry. 'We're nearly at the Mall. You'll see the Palace in a minute.'

They accelerated through an archway on to a big wide road lined with trees.

'There. Up ahead.'

At the end of the road Atticus could see a beautiful building the colour of sand surrounded by tall gates. Buckingham Palace! The last time he'd seen it had been as a tiny dot from the London Eye. He preferred the view down here. Suddenly he felt very important. He was going to meet the Queen! He wished Inspector Cheddar had remembered to give him his police-cat badge back to show Her Majesty.

NEE-NAW. NEE-NAW. NEE-NAW. Within seconds they had arrived.

Two guards in red and black uniform opened the gates. Atticus shrank back when he saw them. They were wearing animals on their heads!

Michael stroked him soothingly. 'Don't worry, Atticus, they're called busbies. It's part of their uniform. They're made of bearskin.'

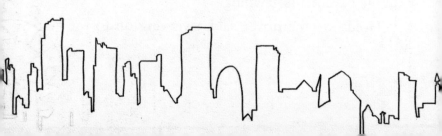

Atticus tried to relax. At least it wasn't cat fur.

The panda car pulled up. *Click!* Callie released Atticus's seat belt. Mrs Cheddar and the kids jumped out to join the two senior policemen and Inspector Cheddar. Atticus milled about their feet, trying not to get trodden on in the excitement.

A tall lady in a smart black suit greeted them. 'I'm Monica Mint, the Queen's private secretary,' she told them. 'Her Majesty is waiting for you. The Prime Minister is here too. There's not a moment to lose.'

She led them into the Palace, her high heels clacking on the marble floor. Atticus barely had time to take in his surroundings as he scampered after her, but he was dimly aware of rich paintings hanging from gilt frames and carved mahogany tables covered in beautiful ornaments and clocks. In his old cat-burgling days he'd have stopped to take a much closer look. Not any more. Now all his attention was focused on saving Her Majesty's wonderful treasure from Zenia Klob and Ginger Biscuit.

Monica Mint paused outside a door. 'Her Majesty will see you now. Ladies, don't forget to curtsy. Gentlemen, remember to bow. Her Majesty considers manners to be most important even at a time of national crisis such as this.'

Atticus felt panicky. He didn't know how to bow! He crept in after the others.

'Ah, there you are, Commissioner.' The Queen was sitting in an armchair by the window holding a cup of tea. Beside her in another armchair, looking worried, sat the Prime Minister.

'Your Majesty.' The Commissioner bowed. 'Prime Minister. You know the Deputy Commissioner already.' The Deputy Commissioner bowed. 'Allow me to introduce the Cheddar family.'

Mrs Cheddar and Callie stepped forward and curtsied. Inspector Cheddar and Michael bowed. Inspector Cheddar lost his balance and banged his head on a table.

'How do you do?' the Queen said.

Inspector Cheddar rubbed his temple. He was about to reply when Monica Mint gave him a dirty look. 'You don't reply to that question,' she hissed.

'And this is their cat, Atticus Claw,' the

Commissioner said.

Atticus tiptoed across the fine carpet towards the Queen. He stood up on his hind legs, placed one paw across his chest and leant forward, trying not to fall over.

'Delighted, I'm sure,' the Queen said. 'I must say you have lovely manners for an animal. Perhaps you could teach the corgis some after tea. Do sit down, everyone.'

Atticus swallowed. He'd just noticed three wiry-looking dogs lying in a basket in the corner of the room watching him hungrily. He hopped on to Mrs Cheddar's lap for safety as they all sat down on a long sofa.

'Atticus helped arrest the Toffly Hall magpie gang, Ma'am,' the Commissioner explained.

'And he knows who Zenia Klob is, Your Majesty,' Michael said. 'He can recognise her even when she's in disguise.'

'How interesting.' The Queen sipped her tea.

'We think Atticus used to work for Zenia Klob, Your Majesty,' Callie said. 'When he was a cat burglar.'

'A cat burglar?' the Queen eyeballed Atticus

disapprovingly. Atticus felt himself blush under his fur.

'He doesn't do it any more, Ma'am,' Mrs Cheddar explained hastily. 'Not since we gave him a home. He's a *reformed* cat burglar now.'

'Well, I'm glad about that,' the Queen said, 'Because we're already short on teaspoons. We sent some off to be cleaned to some people called Toffly and never got them back.' She sighed. 'And we'll be short on everything else if this Klob person has her way.' She turned to the Commissioner. 'What are we going to do? Klob seems to have it all sewn up. If Biscuit eats the ravens, I've had it.'

The Commissioner looked gloomy. 'I don't know,' he admitted.

Inspector Cheddar was gawping at the Queen. His nervousness had got the better of him. 'I have an idea, your Queenliness,' he bellowed suddenly. 'It's to do with Atticus.'

'Spit it out then,' the Prime Minister grumbled. He didn't want the monarchy to fall while he was in charge. The papers would be full of it. He'd never get re-elected.

'I misjudged Atticus, your noble personage,'

Inspector Cheddar squeaked. 'I dragged him away when he was on to Klob at the Tower.'

Atticus began to purr softly. It wasn't often Inspector Cheddar admitted he was wrong or said anything nice about him.

'You mean this is all your fault?' the Prime Minister complained.

'I'm afraid so,' Inspector Cheddar gulped. 'But it's taught me a lesson.'

'What lesson would that be, Inspector?' the Queen asked kindly.

'It's taught me to trust Atticus.'

Atticus's purr grew louder.

'Bit late!' the Prime Minister growled.

'Your point being?' the Queen asked.

'If Atticus really *did* work for Klob, most high and mighty lady . . .' Inspector Cheddar hesitated.

'Go on . . .'

'He might be able to infiltrate the gang,' Inspector Cheddar said quickly. 'Then he'd be able to keep an eye on the ravens just in case Biscuit gets peckish. He could make sure they don't get hurt . . .'

'. . . while we work out a plan to save the Crown

95

Jewels,' the Commissioner finished. He thumped Inspector Cheddar on the back. 'Good thinking, Cheddar!'

Atticus stopped purring. His body went rigid. *Infiltrate the gang?* Were they mad? Ginger Biscuit would eat him alive.

'That's not a bad idea, Cheddar,' the Prime Minister grunted. 'For someone as hopeless as you.'

'Klob said Ginger Biscuit was keeping the ravens somewhere no *human* would ever find them,' the Deputy Commissioner recalled.

'But another *cat* might,' the Commissioner exclaimed, staring at Atticus.

'Especially if he could worm his way into Biscuit's confidence,' the Prime Minister agreed.

Worm his way into Biscuit's confidence? Atticus's good ear drooped. Ginger Biscuit hated other cats, especially Atticus. He wished he could explain to everyone there wasn't a cat's chance in clover that Biscuit would fall for it.

'But it's dangerous,' Callie protested. She picked Atticus up and cuddled him.

'Atticus could get hurt.' Michael stroked his ears.

'I'm not sure we should ask him to do it,' Mrs Cheddar said in a worried voice. 'He'd be taking a terrible risk.'

The Queen put down her cup of tea. 'Monica, bring Atticus to me, please,' she said. 'He and I need to have a little chat.'

Atticus felt strong hands pick him up. Monica Mint carried him over to the Queen's armchair and placed him on a footstool.

'Get me my glasses.'

Monica Mint handed the Queen a leather case.

The Queen leant forward. Gently she took the corner of Atticus's red handkerchief between her fingers. 'Atticus Grammaticus Cattypuss Claw,' she read the spidery writing slowly. 'What a wonderful name! You'd have to be very clever and independent-minded to be given a name like that.'

Atticus began to purr.

'I always think,' the Queen said, 'that animals are highly intelligent. Probably much more so than humans.'

Atticus purred louder. He decided he liked the Queen. She wasn't scary in the least.

'Which is why I'm not going to make you do

97

this if you don't want to,' the Queen said firmly. 'If you choose to volunteer for this mission, that would be absolutely marvellous. However, if you do not wish to infiltrate Klob's ghastly gang and worm your way into this so-called Ginger Biscuit's confidence, then you are completely free not to.'

'But, Your Majesty,' the Prime Minister protested.

'Britain is a free country,' the Queen glared at him. 'People and cats have choices. They cannot be compelled to do things against their will. Which is why Zenia Klob can go and jump off a cliff. With or without her conniving cat.'

'But, Your Majesty!' the Prime Minister gasped. 'If Biscuit kills the ravens, the monarchy will fall.'

'I know that,' the Queen said sharply. 'But I'm not giving in to a ransom demand. And I'm not going to force Atticus to do something he doesn't want to.'

Atticus was gazing at the Queen admiringly. She'd really give up her throne rather than make him go undercover and face Klob and Biscuit? He felt a lump in his throat.

'Monica, you'd better go and pack me a bag,'

the Queen said, turning to her secretary. 'And put a pair of pyjamas and a toothbrush in for Philip. And book us into a B&B would you? There are some nice ones in Scotland. Commissioner, you make contact with Klob and tell her from me to get lost.'

'But, Ma'am!' The Commissioner was on his feet. 'Can't we at least use Atticus to hold Klob and Biscuit off for a bit while we think of something else?'

The Queen put up her hand to silence him. 'I've made my mind up, Commissioner. I'm not negotiating with criminals.'

Atticus could hardly believe it. He'd never have dreamt that the Queen could be so brave. Of course she was right. They shouldn't give in to Klob's demands. They shouldn't let Ginger Biscuit call the shots. And if the Queen could be brave, then so could he. He would do it. He would go undercover and try to keep the ravens safe, however dangerous it was.

'Meow,' he yowled.

'Atticus is trying to say something,' Callie said.

Atticus puffed up his fur. 'Meow,' he cried again.

'I think he wants to tell us he's going to do it!' Michael said. 'Is that what you mean, Atticus?'

'Meow, meow, meow!!!'

'Yippee!' Inspector Cheddar and the two senior policemen high-fived one another.

The Prime Minister helped himself to a chocolate biscuit.

Mrs Cheddar came over and knelt beside Atticus. She stroked his good ear.

'Are you sure, Atticus?' she said gently. Her eyes met the Queen's.

'Meow.'

'Quite, quite sure?' the Queen tickled his chin.

Atticus purred throatily. He'd never been more sure of anything in his life. 'Meow.'

'Then whatever happens, I am eternally grateful to you,' the Queen said. She smiled at Mrs Cheddar. 'And to your family for letting you take this brave step. Monica, get Atticus a sardine, please. He looks hungry.'

'Yes, Ma'am.' Monica Mint hurried off.

'And while Atticus is eating that, the rest of us

had better make a plan.' Her eyes twinkled. 'I think I've got an idea. Prime Minister,' she turned to him, 'do we still have those fake Crown Jewels we had made for my Jubilee dressing-up party?'

'I believe we do, Ma'am.' The Prime Minister grinned.

'Excellent,' the Queen said, nodding. 'Then let's whack them out of the cupboard and get ready to clobber Klob.'

Thug wasn't very pleased. He and the boys – Slasher, Pig, Wally and Gizzard – were still shut in the raven pens. Zenia Klob had disappeared back to the barge to try on disguises. Ginger Biscuit was chatting to Jimmy over a cup of tea in the raven master's hut.

'Why are we still stuck in here, anyway?' Thug complained, ruffling his feathers. 'The Tower's been evacuated like what that old boot wanted. I thought we'd be trying on ermine.'

'What's erming?' Gizzard asked.

'Don't you know anything, Giz?' Thug snorted. 'It's erm-*ine*, not erm-*ing*. And it's a type of fur. It's what the Queen wears for special occasions like getting crowned and stuff.'

'You'd look good in ermine, Thug.' Slasher

nodded. 'Seems a shame not to at least try it!'

'Never mind bloomin' ermine, I need to stretch my wings,' Pig grunted. 'I'm all cooped up, like a hen.'

'It's as bad as the slammer,' Gizzard whined.

'The water's full of bird poo,' Wally moaned.

'That's your fault, Wal!' Slasher snarled.

'Yeah, you're the one with the supercharged poo-packed bum,' Thug agreed.

'CHAKA-CHAKA-CHAKA-CHAKA-CHAKA!' The magpies started to fight.

Ginger Biscuit strolled over. 'What seems to be the problem?' he asked.

'Let us out!' the magpies squawked.

Ginger Biscuit yawned. 'I might,' he said. 'Or I might not. What do you think, Jimmy?'

Jimmy Magpie joined them. 'Can't see the harm,' he said. 'As long as you don't do anything silly.'

'Silly?' Thug cried huffily. 'Us?'

'Like what, Boss?' Slasher demanded.

'Like flying up into the air so that one of the humans can take a pot shot at you,' Jimmy said.

Gizzard gulped. 'I thought all the guards had gone.'

'They have,' Ginger Biscuit said. 'The Queen ordered them out after Zenia's broadcast. But you can bet your beak that somewhere across the river on one of those tall buildings will be a police marksman. You fly up there . . .' he gestured towards the sky, 'and BANG!' He stood up and flapped his paws. Then he drew a claw across his throat. 'Like a turkey at Christmas.'

'We don't want any more funerals, boys,' Jimmy Magpie reminded them solemnly. 'Enough of us magpies have already died at the hands of humans. Remember Beaky, Penguin and Goon?'

Thug gulped. Beaky, Penguin and Goon had got squished by cars. *Very* squished.

'Maybe I don't want to stretch my wings after all,' Pig agreed.

'We could go for a hop instead,' Slasher suggested.

'Yeah, let's do that,' Thug said. 'Can we go see the Crown Jewels, Jimmy, please? Can we?'

'I don't see why not,' Jimmy said expansively. 'Let's all go. See if they've disarmed the security system yet. Come on, Ginger.'

'All right,' Ginger Biscuit agreed, picking the

lock with a claw. 'Then I'll go and give the ravens some more blood.' The pen door swung open. The magpies shoved their way out. Ginger Biscuit leapt onto the ancient wall behind the pens, dropped down the other side and sauntered off to explore with Jimmy hopping beside him. The other magpies followed.

'I really don't like that cat!' Thug whispered.

'I don't know why the Boss listens to him,' Slasher complained. 'It's like he doesn't care about us any more.'

'Imagine the Boss getting in with a cat!' Pig spat.

'And a human!' Wally grumbled.

'I'm fed up with it,' Gizzard agreed. 'We should do something about it.'

'Yeah,' Thug pulled a strangled face. 'Let's get our own back.'

'Chaka-chaka-chaka-chaka-chaka.' The magpies grumbled and mumbled and hopped, all of which proved to be very hard work. They hadn't got very far before they collapsed for a rest on a patch of grass.

''Ere,' said Thug. 'Isn't this Tower Green? Where the doc said they used to chop off people's heads?'

'Oh yeah.' Slasher looked round curiously. 'Can you believe the story about that bloke who had his head sewn back on for the family picture?'

'You'd think it would look a bit odd in a photo,' Thug said doubtfully, 'all that blood dripping out of his neck.'

'They didn't have photos in those days, you moron.' Jimmy was waiting for them. 'They had paintings. They wouldn't have painted the blood.'

'Hurry up,' Ginger Biscuit said. 'It's getting dark.'

Slasher blinked at him. ''Ere, Wal,' he said slowly, 'did you like them ghost stories the doc told?'

'Yeah!' Wally flapped his wings excitedly.

'I loved them!' Thug chattered. 'Especially the one about Anne Boleyn walking round with her head tucked under her arm, moaning!'

106

'Whoooooooo!' Pig cried. 'Whooooooooooooo!'

'Shut up,' Ginger Biscuit said.

Slasher put his head on one side. There was something funny about the way Ginger Biscuit was behaving. 'What about you, Giz?'

'I liked the one about the polar bear rattling its chains,' Gizzard giggled. 'Imagine hearing that in the dark! *Chink-chink!* You'd have more bumps than a goose.'

'Stop it,' Ginger Biscuit said.

'What about the wailing woman?' Slasher suggested. 'She sounded pretty freaky.'

'Whoooooooo!' Pig wailed. 'Whooooooooooooo!'

The magpies hopped about, laughing. Even Jimmy chuckled.

'Belt up!' Ginger Biscuit said.

'My favourite was the heavy tread of the axe man,' Slasher said slyly. 'I mean what if we were all sitting here and we heard that, eh? Like we was about to get our heads chopped off?' He jumped up and down. 'Thump. Thump. Thump.'

'Yeah, is this place spooky or what?' Thug pulled a funny face. 'Especially in the dark.'

'Whoooooo!' It was Pig again. 'Whoooooo!'

'PACK IT IN!' Ginger Biscuit roared.

Slasher winked at Thug. 'Is everything all right?' he asked.

Ginger Biscuit was glancing around nervously.

'Wait a minute, lads,' Thug whispered. 'I do believe he's scared of ghosts.'

'I am not scared of ghosts,' Ginger Biscuit snarled.

'Chink-chink!' Gizzard crept up behind him.

Ginger Biscuit jumped.

'Yeah you are,' Slasher said.

'You're a scaredy-CAT!' Wally sniggered.

'Scaredy-cat! Scaredy-cat! Biscuit is a scaredy-cat!' Pig crowed.

SLASH! Ginger Biscuit's claws raked through the air. He pinned Pig by the tail. 'Say that again, magpie, and it'll be *your* funeral you go to next.'

'Sorry,' Pig gulped.

The other magpies hopped backwards. Slasher tripped over Thug. Thug tripped over Gizzard. Gizzard tripped over Wally. And Wally did a poo which they all slipped over in. 'Chaka-chaka-chaka-chaka-chaka!' The magpies picked themselves up one by one. They pecked and shoved and chattered.

Ginger Biscuit waited until they were quiet. He let go of Pig. 'Now shut it and follow me.'

They made their way across the courtyard to the Jewel House. The door was open.

'Inside.' Ginger Biscuit led the way through a dark room towards some heavy metal doors, which guarded the vault where the Crown Jewels were kept. 'This is it.' He pushed. The magpies tensed themselves, waiting for the screech of the alarm, but there was silence.

'It's off,' Ginger Biscuit said, satisfied. 'Looks like the Queen's seen sense. Once we get this lot on the barge, we'll motor to the airport.'

'Where is the airport?' Jimmy asked.

'Just along the river.' Ginger Biscuit grinned. 'This time tomorrow we'll be in Siberia.'

'Where's that?' Slasher whispered.

'I dunno, but it sounds lovely,' Thug sighed.

'It's one of them holiday places,' Gizzard said. 'Where you get a sun tan.'

'Oooooh!' Thug waggled his tail. 'Can I get a cocktail with an umbrella and a cherry on a stick?'

'Let's make up a new one,' Pig suggested. 'A special magpie cocktail.'

'What about a Poo Colada?' Wally chuckled.

'Nice one, Wal.' The magpies started to chatter.

Ginger Biscuit pushed the door open fully and walked into the vault. All at once the room was flooded with light.

'CHAKA-CHAKA-CHAKA-CHAKA-CHAKA!' The magpies hopped about in panic.

'They're automatic,' Ginger called. 'Nothing to worry about. Come on.'

The magpies followed him inside.

Thug stopped dead. 'It's so beautiful,' he sighed, gazing at the glass cases full of precious treasure.

'Look at the crowns!' Jimmy's eyes glittered.

'And the sceptres!' Slasher gawped.

'And the orbs!' Gizzard gasped.

'And the bracelets!' Wally wailed.

'And the rings!' Pig snorted.

'And the ermine!' Thug started to cry. 'I think I've died and gone to magpie fashion heaven.'

THWUMP!

'What was that?' Ginger Biscuit swallowed.

The magpies looked round fearfully.

'It's the axe man!' Slasher screeched, hiding behind Jimmy. 'It's his heavy tread! He's come to chop us!'

'Quick! Over here!' Ginger Biscuit scampered behind one of the glass cabinets. The magpies fluttered after him. They peered out from their hiding place.

A huge humped shadow spread across the wall.

'Hello, Ginger,' a voice said.

'It's you it wants!' Thug cried, giving Ginger a shove.

'I'm not going anywhere.' Ginger Biscuit dug his claws in. He was shaking.

'Shut up, Thug,' Jimmy pecked the magpie on the head. 'Ghosts can't talk. Anyway, I recognise that voice. It's not the axe man.'

'Hello?' the voice called.

'SSSSSSSSSS! So do I,' Ginger Biscuit snarled. He stalked out from behind the cabinet. The magpies hopped cautiously after him.

A brown-and-black-striped tabby with four white paws and a chewed ear stood in front of them, a red handkerchief around his neck.

'Claw,' Ginger Biscuit hissed. 'I had a feeling you might show up sooner or later.'

'You've got a nerve turning up like this,' Jimmy spat.
'After what you did at Toffly Hall.'

'What do you want?' Ginger Biscuit growled.

Atticus swallowed. It had been easy enough to
creep past the gang on Tower Green and hide in
the Jewel House. It had even been fun watching
Ginger Biscuit squirm with fear when he thought
Atticus was a ghost. Now came the hard part. He
needed Ginger Biscuit's respect; and the only way
to get it was to tough it out. He shot out a paw and
pinned the nearest magpie.

'I thought you said he was a pampered pet,
Boss!' Pig squawked.

Atticus gripped Pig tightly. 'No chance,' he
hissed. 'I'm back to burgling. And if you call me

that again I'll pull all your tail feathers out one by one and roast you in boiling oil.'

Pig fainted.

'I don't believe you, Claw,' Jimmy said. 'You double-crossed us last time. To save your own skin.'

Atticus kicked Pig out of the way with his back paw and advanced on Thug. 'You said it, Jimmy. I had to save my own skin. That's what you'd expect from the world's greatest cat burglar, isn't it? Besides, I thought it was *you* who double-crossed *me*.'

Atticus saw a shadow of doubt pass across Jimmy's face. It was going better than he'd hoped. Jimmy was feeding him all the right lines. He prayed it was making an impression on Ginger Biscuit. His paw shot out and pinned Thug.

'Why me?' Thug cawed weakly. 'Why not Slasher?'

'Don't worry, he's next.' Atticus patted Thug from side to side across the floor, like a fat feathery ball. 'Look at it from my point of view, Jimmy,' he continued reasonably. 'The only way I could be sure of getting out of Littleton-on-Sea was by cosying up to the Cheddars and *pretending* to help them catch you and your gang.' The words tasted bitter in Atticus's mouth. None of it was true and it made him feel disloyal to the Cheddars. He loved all of them, especially Callie and Michael. But he had to go through with it. He had to gain the gang's trust. He'd promised the Queen.

'You're saying you're not a pet?' Ginger Biscuit demanded.

Atticus looked him in the eye. With one sweep of his paw he sent Thug hurtling towards the ermine.

CRUMP!

'Me?' he laughed. 'A pet?! Come on, Ginger, you know me better than that. Get real! How could a cat trained by Zenia Klob ever become a *pet*?!' He pinned Slasher. 'Once a cat burglar, always a cat burglar: that's what I say.'

'I still don't buy it,' Jimmy grumbled.

'Help me!' Slasher sobbed. 'Somebirdy help me!'

'I don't care whether you buy it or not, Jimmy,' Atticus hissed. 'You're just a *bird*. This is between us *cats*.' He held Slasher up by the tail.

Ginger Biscuit laughed. 'You've toughened up, Atticus, since the last time I saw you.'

'You'd better believe it.' Atticus bared his teeth at Jimmy. 'And I don't take orders from magpies.' He pinged Slasher at the orbs.

'Neither do I,' Ginger Biscuit said lazily. 'That looks like fun,' he added, as Slasher slid down the glass cabinet. 'Mind if I join you?'

'Be my guest,' Atticus said, wondering what he'd do if Ginger Biscuit mangled the remaining magpies.

'Who wants to be next?' Ginger grinned.

Gizzard and Wally went pale.

Ginger Biscuit gathered them up. '*Both* your turns!' he sniggered. The magpies sailed through the air towards the crowns.

CRUNCH! SPLAT!

'Stop throwing my magpies!' Jimmy hopped about furiously. 'We're a team, remember? CHAKA-CHAKA-CHAKA-CHAKA-CHAKA.'

'Shut up, Jimmy,' Ginger Biscuit said, 'unless you want to join them. Atticus is right. You're getting too big for your little birdy boots. It's the cats who call the shots around here, not the magpies.'

He padded over to Atticus and put a paw around his shoulder. 'That was an impressive piece of burgling you pulled off in Toffany's the other day,' he purred.

For a moment Atticus was puzzled. Then he realised. Ginger Biscuit had made the same mistake as Inspector Cheddar. He thought Atticus was *stealing* the ring when they saw one another at the jewellery shop.

'Thanks,' Atticus growled. Getting a compliment from Ginger Biscuit was like eating your own sick. He could hardly stomach it. But he had to. 'Old habits die hard,' he said. 'Zenia trained us well.'

'She wasn't too happy when you scratched her,' Ginger Biscuit withdrew his paw.

Atticus shrugged. 'It was an accident. I was desperate to get away from the Cheddars.'

'I don't blame you,' Ginger said. 'They sound a real bunch of pathetic suck-ups: the sort of people who won't let you spit out mouse guts at the table.'

'Yeah,' Atticus agreed through gritted teeth, hating him. 'That's what they're like. But I don't want to talk about them. Let's just concentrate on the reason I came.'

'Which is?' Ginger raised an eyebrow.

'I want in.'

'CHAKA-CHAKA-CHAKA-CHAKA-CHAKA!'

Ginger Biscuit silenced Jimmy with a look. He turned his pale blue eyes on to Atticus. 'It's okay by me,' he said eventually. 'I'd even say I'm quite glad to see you. I'm sick of jailbirds for company. I'll take you to Zenia. But I'm telling you, Atticus, she was pretty mad.'

'Why don't I bring her a present?' Atticus asked quickly, remembering the Queen's plan.

'All right,' Ginger Biscuit agreed. He glanced around at the glittering jewels. 'You choose.'

'What about the alarm?' Atticus asked.

'It's off.'

'I'll take one of the crowns,' Atticus said, advancing towards a cabinet. 'But I'll need something to stand on.'

'How about this?' Ginger Biscuit pushed a heavy chair across the floor. His muscles rippled.

'Thanks!' *What a show-off!* Atticus thought. *Just like in the old days.* 'Here will do.' He leapt on to the chair and pretended to examine the lock. 'Piece of steak!' he announced, pinging out the claws of his right front paw. Delicately he began to pick at it. There was complete silence in the room. *Any minute now* . . . Atticus tried to look as if he was concentrating. 'Got it,' he said. The lock snapped open.

BBRBRBRBRBRBRRBRBRBRBRBRBRBRBRBRB RBRBRBRBRBRBRBRBRBRBRBRBRBRBRBRBRBRBR BRBRBRBRBRBRBRBRBB BRBRBRRBRBRBRBRBR BRBRBRBRBRBRBRBRBRBRBRBRBRBRBRBRBRB

Ginger Biscuit and the magpies looked around wildly.

BINGO! Atticus breathed a sigh of relief. Everything was going according to plan. So far.

'Quick!' he shouted. 'The vault doors are closing!'

He raced towards the exit, Ginger Biscuit and the magpies hard on his heels.

CLANG. CLUNK. CLANG. CLUNK! The doors shut behind them.

'Phew!' Atticus gasped. He put his paws to his ears. The alarm was still screaming. 'I thought you said it was off!' he shouted.

'I thought it was!' Ginger Biscuit snarled. 'Zenia won't like this one little bit! Come on.'

Atticus followed Ginger Biscuit out of the Jewel House, the alarm still ringing in his ears. It was the signal for phase two of the Queen's plan.

They re-crossed the courtyard and followed the ancient wall through the archway and back to the cobbled street. The magpies hopped and fluttered behind them, squawking furiously.

'Where are we going?' Atticus asked. The ravens had to be somewhere in the Tower. The question was, where?

'You'll see.' Ginger Biscuit sniffed the air. 'This way.' He crossed the street, slipped under a railing and padded down some stone steps. Atticus followed reluctantly. *Why were they heading for the river?* The ravens couldn't be there. He began to worry that Ginger Biscuit intended to drown him.

He had to go on, though. There was no turning back now. The magpies tumbled after him.

At the bottom of the steps was a landing point. It was filled with shallow green water. Beyond that was a gate to the Thames. It had a notice on the top.

TRAITORS' GATE

'This is where they brought the prisoners by boat in the old days before they were executed for treason,' Ginger Biscuit explained casually.

'You'd better watch out, Claw,' Jimmy cawed softly, 'Or you'll be next.'

The tide was out. They sloshed through the water and squeezed through the bars to the bank of the river.

'There.' Ginger Biscuit pointed at a dark shape a little way along the river bank.

The barge! *Of course.* It was exactly the sort of dingy, stinking place that Zenia Klob would hole up in. Atticus should have realised it belonged to her when he first saw it that morning through the door near the portcullis.

He picked his way through the mud after Ginger Biscuit. It sucked at his white paws, making them black and brown like the rest of him. The magpies hopped after them, leaving prints. Eventually, they reached the barge.

'Up you go.' Ginger Biscuit pointed to a step-ladder.

Atticus scrambled up, his muddy feet slipping on the slimy treads. When he got to the rail he jumped down on to the deck.

The magpies fluttered beside him.

'Zenia's inside.' Ginger Biscuit held the cabin door open for Atticus.

Atticus stalked in, keeping his tail high.

Zenia Klob had her Mildred Molotov outfit on. She barely seemed to notice Atticus. She paced the cabin, swearing in Russian at the top of her voice,

flicking hairpins at a dartboard. On the table was a green bottle marked SLEEPING POTION. Beside it stood a half-empty bottle of Thumpers' Traditional Black – the dye she'd used on the magpies' raven suits.

Atticus peered at the label. *55 Tower Vaults,* he read. Tower Vaults was where he'd seen the fish-and-chip shop. Zenia didn't have to go far for supplies.

'I'm terribly sorry, Miss Klob, for the mix-up in the Jewel House. There was an electrical malfunction.'

Atticus jumped. It was the Police Commissioner's voice. Zenia had her phone on speaker. The Commissioner was talking to her from the Palace. Phase Two of the Queen's plan was in full swing. All Atticus had to do now was make sure the ravens were safe. The Cheddars would do the rest. Then, at midnight, once the villains thought they'd got what they wanted, Atticus and the Cheddars would make their getaway together.

'It's Ms, not Miss,' Zenia shouted. 'And vot do you mean an electrical malfunction? I told you to turn the alarm off. Or else.' *THWACK!* One of the hairpins bounced off the board and landed on Thug. 'Vot part of "or else" don't you understand, you idiot?'

'I'm thinking of giving up a life of crime!' Thug keeled over.

'Her Majesty is sending you a team of electricians straight away,' the Commissioner said smoothly. 'They should be with you any time now. They'll be in a white van. I'm sure they'll have it all sorted out for you in a jiffy so you can carry on with your evil plot to steal the nation's treasure.'

'They'd better,' Zenia snarled. 'If you and the Queen ever vant to see those ravens again.' She slammed down the phone. 'Atticus?' Zenia's beady black eyes finally focused on him. 'Vot are you doing here?'

'Meow.' Summoning all his courage Atticus walked over to Zenia Klob and rubbed his whiskers on her hobnail boots.

'So, you missed me, did you?' Zenia bent down to stroke him. 'Don't you think that's sveet, Ginger?'

Ginger Biscuit gave a brief MMYYAAWW, which could have meant yes or no. It would be just like Ginger Biscuit, Atticus thought, to say one thing to his face and rip his throat out when Zenia was around. He wondered if it was a trap after all.

'Vell, I don't!' Zenia grabbed him by the scruff of his neck.

Atticus dangled helplessly in front of her. Zenia had hold of the knot of his handkerchief. She was choking him. He could hear the magpies chuckling in the cabin behind him. 'Chaka-chaka-chaka-chaka-chaka.' This was what Jimmy and his gang had hoped for. Even Thug had woken up to have a look.

'You scratched me, you little beast,' Zenia said, eyeing him nastily. 'I've a good mind to let Biscuit kill you. You'd like that, vouldn't you, Biscuit? Now you're out of rats. I suppose that's vy you brought Atticus to me? You vere feeling a bit peckish.'

Atticus retched. His eyes popped.

There was a flash of ginger fur. *SHWIPP!* Atticus fell to the ground. His shredded handkerchief drifted down beside him in two pieces.

'If you're going to do it inside, Ginger, make sure you don't make a mess,' Zenia Klob said in a bored tone. 'Blood is very difficult to get out of carpet.'

Atticus braced himself. He knew he didn't stand a chance if Ginger Biscuit attacked him, but he wasn't going down without a fight. To his amazement, however, Ginger Biscuit retreated to the sofa, took off his collar and reached for the sleeping potion bottle. He started to dip the studs.

Zenia Klob looked at Ginger Biscuit, astonished. 'Don't tell me you're going soft, Biscuit. It's not like *you* to give someone another chance.'

Ginger Biscuit growled.

Zenia Klob shrugged. 'Okay, have it your vay. You might be right. Ve could use an extra pair of paws. Or, more importantly, an extra set of *claws*.' She prodded Atticus with the steel toe of her boot. 'Especially now I've decided to kill the ravens anyway, even if the Queen *does* meet my demands.'

Atticus froze.

Ginger Biscuit started to purr. He stretched and rolled.

'I'd thought you'd like that, Biscuit. It'll teach our enemies not to try our patience with electrical malfunctions!' Zenia Klob cackled. 'The Municipal

Republic of Great Britain! I'd love to see the look on Her Majesty's face ven that happens. I think I'll put on some revolutionary marching music to celebrate. Let's burn the beetroot, boys! Ve're having a party!'

Atticus's ears drooped. Not at the revolutionary marching music or the smell of burning beetroot, although that was bad enough. It was because Zenia Klob had decided to kill the ravens anyway! That wasn't in the Queen's brilliant plan. Atticus felt a surge of panic. He didn't know what to do.

Ginger Biscuit laid his collar carefully on the table to dry. He dropped down off the sofa and strolled over to Atticus. 'Lucky for you I'm feeling generous, comrade,' he hissed in his ear. 'Or you'd be dead.'

'Yeah, thanks,' Atticus muttered.

'Want to know why I did it?' Ginger Biscuit asked slyly.

'Why did you?' Atticus said. He had a sinking feeling in his stomach.

'I'm going to set you a test.' Ginger replied. 'I'm going to let *you* kill the ravens. That way you can prove to me you really have changed.'

'What happens if I refuse?' Atticus said. 'You . . . I mean we . . . are going to get the Crown Jewels anyway. We don't need to kill the ravens. It's a waste of time.'

'Oh, Atticus,' Ginger Biscuit covered him with a puff of rat-smelling breath. 'That's exactly the sort of loose talk that can get you into trouble. Anyone would think you didn't *want* to kill them.' He shook his head sadly. 'I hear drowning is very unpleasant. Especially for a cat.'

'CHAKA-CHAKA-CHAKA-CHAKA! Drown him! Drown him! Drown him!' The magpies chanted, hopping up and down.

Somehow Atticus managed a laugh. 'I was just kidding,' he said. He pinged out his claws like he'd seen Ginger do – one at a time, slowly. POP. POP. POP. POP. 'Show me where you're keeping them,' he said, gritting his teeth. 'I can't wait to get started.'

Ginger Biscuit and Atticus retraced their muddy steps towards Traitors' Gate. Zenia had ordered the magpies to remain with her. The tide was turning and the two cats had to paddle most of the way. Atticus could hear the water sloshing around the bottom of the gate.

'Hurry up,' Ginger Biscuit urged. 'We need to get to the steps before the tide gets any higher.'

Atticus's tummy was already wet. The tide was coming in fast now. 'How will you . . . I mean, we . . . load the jewels?' he asked.

'Simple,' Ginger Biscuit replied. 'Zenia will open Traitors' Gate and float the barge up to the steps.'

'Aren't you worried the cops will come after you . . . I mean, us . . . if we kill the ravens?' Atticus was trying desperately to think of a way to stop them.

'They'll never catch us.' Ginger Biscuit grinned. 'That barge goes like a rocket. Zenia's had it kitted out with the latest Russian turbo-charged engine.'

Atticus dragged behind, his feet slurping in the mud. 'You sure it's safe?' he asked.

'Stop worrying, Atticus!' Ginger Biscuit sounded exasperated. 'Zenia's got it covered. She's been training for this operation for months. There's nothing we're not prepared for,' he boasted.

Except ghosts, Atticus thought suddenly, remembering the conversation he'd overheard on Tower Green.

They squeezed through Traitors' Gate and scampered up the steps.

'This way,' Ginger Biscuit said. He headed back across the cobbles and through the archway, then veered sharply to the left.

Atticus already knew where he was going. He should have realised sooner. It was just the sort of place Biscuit would choose to hide the ravens.

BLOODY TOWER

'Quite a good name for it, really,' Ginger Biscuit joked, 'considering what we have in mind.'

What YOU have in mind, you mean, Atticus thought grimly.

'They're in here.' Ginger Biscuit led the way up a short spiral staircase. Atticus's eyes adjusted to the darkness. They were in a large empty room with heavy curtains tied back with rope.

Ginger Biscuit sauntered towards a recess in the corner of the room.

Atticus thought it was a fireplace. 'What are you doing?' he demanded. 'They're not up the chimney, are they?' He tried a laugh. 'That would be a stupid place to put a raven. You sure they haven't flown away?'

'Yeah, I'm sure,' Ginger Biscuit snapped. 'The Queen's still on the throne, isn't she? Besides,' he grinned at Atticus, as though he had a nasty secret he was about to share, 'this isn't a fireplace.'

'What is it then?' Atticus stared in surprise.

'It's a loo.' There was a grating noise as Ginger Biscuit pulled the cover to one side. 'It's what they used to call a garderobe. Have a look.'

'No thanks!' Atticus pulled a face. He liked a

little privacy when he went to the loo. He couldn't imagine doing it there.

'Not squeamish, are you?' Ginger taunted.

Atticus ignored him. 'Where are the ravens, then?'

'At the bottom,' Ginger said. 'I threw them down after we'd switched them with the magpies. One after the other. Plop. Plop. Plop.' He chuckled.

Atticus ignored him. 'How are we going to get them out to kill them?'

'We're not,' Ginger grinned. 'You're going down after them.'

'I'm not going down there,' Atticus said at once. 'You don't even know where it comes out.'

'Yes I do,' Ginger hissed. 'It ends up in a sort of poo bunker. I think the river used to sluice it out when the moat was full, but it doesn't come up that far any more. Either that or someone shovelled it out. Don't worry,' he added, seeing the look on Atticus's face, 'it's clean now.'

'How am I going to get out once I've mashed them?' Atticus felt a rising sense of panic. He didn't like confined spaces.

'You can either climb back up again,' Ginger

Biscuit said, flexing his muscles. 'Like I do. Or you can get out into the moat.'

'The moat?' Atticus repeated.

'Yeah, that's how I found it in the first place,' Ginger Biscuit boasted. 'I was out ratting when I came across an old pipe. I followed it until I reached the poo bunker, then I climbed up the poo hole to see where it came out.' He picked a match up off the floor and chewed it. 'Zenia gave me the job of hiding the ravens where no *human* would ever think to look. I decided this was the perfect place.' Ginger Biscuit laughed. 'Who's going to want to investigate an ancient toilet? Except Wally, of course,' he added.

'No one,' Atticus said. 'It's brilliant.' An idea was beginning to form in his mind. The poo hole led to the bunker. The bunker led to the pipe. The pipe led to the moat. And from the moat it was just a short dash to Tower Vaults and Thumpers' Traditional Dye shop. If he could only get there and back without Ginger Biscuit or the magpies knowing, then he might still be able to save the ravens.

Atticus stalked over to the poo hole and sniffed

delicately. A current of air wafted up. It smelt damp but not dirty. 'Okay,' he said. 'I'll do it.' Gripping on to the edge with his front paws, Atticus lowered his hind legs into the shaft. He scrabbled for a foot-hold, but the sides of the shaft were smooth.

'It's not much of a drop,' Ginger's face loomed over him. 'And anyway, you've still got eight lives left.' He put a paw out. Atticus ducked his head. Ginger Biscuit's claws brushed his chewed ear. 'For now.'

For a split second Atticus wondered if it was a trick. Were the ravens really hidden here? Or had Ginger Biscuit lured him to the Bloody Tower to kill him by dropping him down an ancient royal toilet into a four-hundred-year-old pile of putrid poo? It would be just the sort of revolting death Ginger Biscuit would dream up! Atticus felt his front paws start to slip. Just then he heard a faint sound from below.

'Waaarrrk!'

It was the ravens.

Atticus closed his eyes. He released his grip. He felt himself plummeting down into the cool earth.

CRUNCH! He landed with a thud. Checking he

hadn't broken anything, he picked himself up slowly and looked about. He was in a small stone cave, somewhere beneath the Tower: its sides were worn smooth from the time when the water from the moat rushed in and out with the tide. A rusty pipe of about half a metre in diameter opened into it. Opposite him, tethered to a rock, were the six ravens. It was just as Biscuit had described.

'Don't kill them yet,' Ginger Biscuit's voice echoed down the shaft. 'We need to wait for the electricians. Once we've got the jewels on board the barge, I'll give you the word.'

'Where are you going now?' Atticus called up.

'Back to the barge to help Zenia,' Biscuit shouted. 'Remember, Atticus, if you don't do the job, I'll do it myself.'

The ravens looked at Atticus dolefully. It seemed like all the fight had gone out of them. They probably hadn't eaten since the morning, Atticus reflected. And being stuffed down a poo hole and tied to a rock by a large ginger tomcat wasn't good for any bird's morale.

'And then I'll kill *you*.' Ginger Biscuit's voice faded away.

There was silence in the cave. Atticus waited until he was sure Ginger Biscuit had gone and then advanced on the ravens. He stopped in front of the biggest one and popped out his claws.

'You heard what your pal said!' the raven squawked. 'You're not supposed to kill us yet.'

'Don't worry,' Atticus whispered. 'He's not my pal. And I'm not going to kill you. I'm going to get you out of here. But you have to promise you'll help me save the monarchy . . . er . . .'

'Georgina,' the big raven introduced herself. 'Of course we promise,' she agreed. 'But how? We wouldn't stand a chance against ginger chops in a fight.'

'We're not going to give him a fight,' Atticus said calmly. 'We're going to give him a *fright*.'

The ravens stared at him.

'Ginger Biscuit is afraid of ghosts,' Atticus explained. 'When he gives me the signal to kill you, *I'm* going to pretend that I've done it. Then *you're* going to pretend to be ghosts.'

'He'll never fall for that!' Georgina said. 'Ghosts are white. We're black.'

'Not for long, you're not,' Atticus grinned. He

released the ravens one by one. 'Wait here until I get back,' he ordered. 'I'll be as quick as I can.'

'Where are you going?' the Georgina asked.

'To get a bottle of Thumpers' Traditional White Beard Dye,' Atticus grinned.

'Beard dye?!' The ravens croaked.

'Don't worry,' Atticus said. 'It also works on feathers. You'll be the scariest ghosts the Tower of London has ever seen!'

'Waarrrk!' The ravens began to crow excitedly.

'We're going to give Ginger Biscuit the fright of his furry life!' Atticus climbed into the opening of the pipe and disappeared.

The white electricians' van trundled across the bridge over the moat towards the Tower. The driver opened the window. 'Raise the portcullis!' he shouted. 'We've come to disarm the security system.'

There was a clunking and grinding as the huge metal grille was winched upwards. The van driver swallowed. Lethal-looking spikes poked down from the bottom like a row of giant daggers.

'Watch out, Dad,' a voice from the back of the van warned, 'in case she drops it on the van.'

'That's what they used to do in the old days,' another voice whispered. 'Then they'd pour boiling oil all over you.'

'Shhh,' the person in the passenger seat put a finger to her lips. 'Let Dad do the talking.'

The van trundled on along the cobbled street past the opening that Atticus and Ginger Biscuit had recently passed through. It turned left through a second archway, wide enough for a vehicle. The driver inched his way towards the Jewel House and stopped the van. 'This is it,' he whispered. 'Ready?'

The three passengers nodded. Quietly the four electricians, dressed in baggy blue overalls and matching baseball caps pulled down over their ears, got out of the van. They began to unload large plastic toolboxes from the back.

'Where is she?' the driver whispered, picking up two of the boxes and carting them up the steps.

'I'M OVER HERE!' Zenia Klob's voice rang round the courtyard. 'VERE YOU CAN'T SEE ME!'

'She's using a megaphone!' the second electrician hissed.

'YOU'RE RIGHT: I *AM* USING A MEGA-PHONE. *AND* MY SUPER-RECEPTIVE HEARING AID, WHICH IS VY I CAN HEAR EVERYTHING YOU SAY.' The cackle came again. 'VOT'S IN THE BOXES?' Zenia Klob demanded.

'Tools!' the driver shouted back. 'We need them to sort out the electrical malfunction.'

'YOU'D BETTER NOT BE LYING,' Zenia Klob yelled, 'OR IT'LL BE YOU THAT'LL HAVE A MALFUNCTION.'

'We're not lying!' the driver yelled back. He hoped Zenia Klob couldn't see his fingers were crossed behind his back. 'The Queen sent us.' He turned to the others. 'Come on, royal team.'

The other electricians followed him towards the Jewel House.

'NOT SO FAST, SPARKY!' Zenia screeched. 'YOU NEED TO VAIT FOR BISCUIT. HE'S COMING VITH YOU TO MAKE SURE YOU DON'T TRY ANYTHING FUNNY.'

The driver swallowed. 'I . . . er . . .' he mumbled.

'VOT VOS THAT YOU SAID? I DIDN'T QUITE CATCH IT.'

'HE CAN'T!' the second electrician shouted

139

hastily. 'No cats allowed on the premises while we're working.'

'VY NOT?' Zenia Klob sounded suspicious.

'HEALTH AND SAFETY,' the third electrician bawled.

'SORRY, SHORTY?' Zenia Klob shrilled. 'I'M GETTING A LOT OF INTERFERENCE IN MY HEARING AID. THE MEGAPHONE SEEMS TO BE SPOILING THE SUPER-RECEPTION.'

The electricians glanced at one another.

'Think of something!' the driver mouthed. 'Quick!'

'HE MIGHT GET ELECTRI-CATTED,' the fourth electrician yelled.

'*!*!*!*!*!*!*!*!*!*!*!*!*!*!*!*!*' Zenia Klob let out a string of rude-sounding Russian words. There was a tense silence. 'VERY VELL,' Zenia said eventually. 'GET ON VITH IT. BUT DON'T TAKE ALL NIGHT. I'M GOING TO FIX MY SUPER-RECEPTIVE HEARING AID. AND THEN I'VE GOT SOME CROWN JEWELS TO STEAL!'

The electricians disappeared inside the Jewel House with the boxes and closed the door behind them. They ripped off their caps.

'Phew!' Inspector Cheddar leaned against the door with a sigh of relief.

'That was close!' sighed Mrs Cheddar.

'I thought she was going to hairpin us,' Michael said.

'I'm glad Ginger Biscuit didn't show up,' Callie breathed.

Inspector Cheddar looked at his watch. It was a few minutes past midnight. 'We'd better get on with it.'

They walked towards the vault. CLANG. CLUNK. CLANG. CLUNK. The heavy metal doors swung open.

'It's lucky Klob didn't work out that these can be controlled from Buckingham Palace!' Mrs Cheddar whispered.

'We don't have much time.' Inspector Cheddar started unpacking the toolboxes. 'If she thinks we've disarmed the system she'll be in here like a bullet.' He took out a sceptre and an orb identical to the ones in the display cabinets. 'Now, let's get these fake jewels into the cabinets and the real ones into the toolboxes.' He picked up the orb and squinted at it. 'It was a brilliant plan of Her

Majesty's to switch them, especially after what Klob did with the ravens and the magpies! Thank goodness she had some fake ones made for her Jubilee dressing-up party.'

'Where's Atticus?' Michael sounded worried. 'He's supposed to meet us here.'

'You do think he's all right, don't you, Mum?' Callie said anxiously.

'I'm sure he's fine,' Mrs Cheddar said. 'He'll be here in a minute. He knows the plan.' She took a skeleton key from her pocket and got to work. Soon all the cabinets were unlocked.

Quickly and quietly the Cheddars took the real Crown Jewels out of the display cabinets and sub-stituted the fake ones. The last thing to be switched was the ermine coronation gown.

'Do you think it will fool Klob?' Mrs Cheddar asked, smoothing down the fake fur collar on the dummy.

'Definitely,' Inspector Cheddar said. 'She won't notice until she gets to Siberia.'

'I'm really worried about Atticus,' Callie said anxiously.

'Me too,' said Michael. 'He should be here by now.'

'I expect he's waiting by the van.' Mrs Cheddar began to re-lock the cabinets.

Inspector Cheddar looked around. 'Now let's pack up the real Crown Jewels and get out of here.'

Hastily they scooped the priceless treasures into the plastic toolboxes and rammed down the lids.

The four Cheddars pushed their baseball caps back on to their heads and made their way out of the vault.

They went down the steps and back out into the night.

'We've finished, Ms Klob,' Inspector Cheddar panted. 'The electrical malfunction's fixed.'

There was no reply.

'It's fine for you to steal the Crown Jewels now,' he wheezed, plonking the heavy toolboxes down on the road beside the van.

There was silence.

'Go ahead,' he added. 'Be our guests.'

Nothing.

'Where is she, Dad?' Michael whispered.

'I don't know.' Inspector Cheddar opened the rear doors of the van and heaved the toolboxes in. The van sank down on its axles. *SSSSSSSSSSSSSS!*

143

There was a loud hissing noise.

'What was that?' Mrs Cheddar said.

Inspector Cheddar had gone pale. 'Sounds like a flat tyre,' he said.

'Make that four flat tyres,' Michael crouched down and looked under the van.

'And no Atticus,' Callie sniffed. 'He's still not here.'

'How did that happen?' Inspector Cheddar scratched his baseball cap.

'Never mind how it happened, darling,' Mrs Cheddar said. 'The question is what are we going to do about it?'

'I'll stay here and guard the Crown Jewels,' Inspector Cheddar said. 'You three get back to the Palace and tell the Commissioner what's happened. Get him to send a recovery truck. If Klob shows up I'll tell her we've had a breakdown and that I've got to wait for the AA.'

'But darling,' Mrs Cheddar protested, 'what if she hairpins you?'

'It doesn't matter,' Inspector Cheddar said bravely. 'As long as she doesn't find out we've switched the Crown Jewels until she's on that plane to Siberia.'

'Where's Atticus?' Callie began to cry.

'Maybe we'll find him on the way out.' Michael swallowed his tears back.

They were both thinking the same thing. *What if Biscuit had harmed him?*

Mrs Cheddar took their hands. 'I'm sure Atticus will be here soon,' she said firmly. 'He's bound to see us walking out. And if he doesn't, Dad will be waiting for him. Now come on, let's go and get some help.' They set off towards the exit. It wasn't long before they disappeared and Inspector Cheddar was left all alone.

16

SSSQQQUUUEEEEAAAAKKK! TRUNDLE-TRUNDLE!
SSSQQQUUUEEEEAAAAKKK! TRUNDLE-TRUNDLE.

Inspector Cheddar looked about nervously. He knew all about the ghosts at the Tower from the guidebook. He swallowed. It didn't sound like the heavy tread of the axe man's footsteps. It certainly wasn't the wailing woman or the chink-chink of the polar bear's chains. And he didn't think a headless Anne Boleyn would make much noise at all. His imagination began to work overtime. Could it be the ghostly cart, which was used to bring prisoners to the executioner's block? Or, even worse, the wheelbarrow they put their bodies in once they'd been beheaded? Or the scraping of old ladies' knitting needles while they gathered to

146

watch the heads tumble? *No. No. No!* he told himself. *You're getting mixed up with the French Revolution.*

'Get a grip on yourself, Cheddar.' He gave himself a smack.

SSSQQQUUUEEEAAAKK! TRUNDLE-TRUNDLE!
SSSQQQUUUEEEAAAKKK! TRUNDLE-TRUNDLE.

The noise came again. Inspector Cheddar began to shake. He went so white he could have been a ghost himself. Something was out there. He wasn't imagining it.

'What do you want?' he quavered.

SSSQQQUUUEEEAAAKK! TRUNDLE-TRUNDLE!
SSSQQQUUUEEEAAAKKK! TRUNDLE-TRUNDLE.

'I'm a yellow belt at karate.' He practised a few wobbly chops.

SSSQQQUUUEEEAAAKK! TRUNDLE-TRUNDLE!
SSSQQQUUUEEEAAAKKK! TRUNDLE-TRUNDLE.

'Reveal yourself in the name of the law,' he demanded in a weak voice. 'I am a . . .' He'd been about to say 'police officer' but remembered just in time not to in case Zenia Klob was out there somewhere, listening on her super-receptive hearing aid. '. . . royal electrician of Buckingham Palace,' he finished lamely.

SSSQQQUUUEEEAAAKK! TRUNDLE-TRUNDLE!
SSSQQQUUUEEEAAAKKK! TRUNDLE-TRUNDLE.

Inspector Cheddar was just about to faint when a large cleaning cart complete with two bins and some brushes loomed into view. It was pushed by a wizened janitor with a bald head, who was dressed in bright orange dungarees and a reflective jacket.

The cart made its way towards the van.

'You look like you could use some *help*,' the janitor said, looking at the van meaningfully. 'From a *friend.*'

To Inspector Cheddar's surprise the janitor winked at him.

'I . . . er . . .'

'It looks like you've got some *very valuable tools* in there,' the janitor said, peering through the window of the van.

'Well . . . er . . .'

'You vouldn't vant anyone to *steal* them, vould you?' The janitor looked about furtively.

An idea dawned on Inspector Cheddar. 'Did the Queen send you?' he whispered excitedly.

The janitor nodded.

'What should we do?' Inspector Cheddar hissed.

'Shhhhh,' the janitor hissed back. 'Klob might be listening. I've got instructions.' He produced a crumpled piece of paper from his overall pocket and handed it to Inspector Cheddar. Then he produced a torch and switched it on. Inspector Cheddar peered at the note.

Give the janitor the real jewels.

Or else.

Signed,

The Queen.
And the corgis.

'Or else what?' Inspector Cheddar whispered, puzzled. It wasn't the sort of note he'd have expected the Queen to write, although the corgis might have.

'Or else Klob might vork out you've switched the real Crown Jewels for fake ones and hairpin you,' the janitor said impatiently. 'Now hurry up, I haven't got all night.'

Inspector Cheddar hesitated for a moment. Then he decided it must be another of the Queen's brilliant plans. Sending a pretend janitor as back-up just in case the van broke down was a stroke of royal genius. He started to unload the toolboxes from the back of the van.

'Put them in that one!' the janitor barked, pointing at one of the two rubbish bins. 'The other one's full.'

Inspector Cheddar heaved them into the empty bin.

'Come on, come on,' the janitor muttered impatiently. 'Places to go, people to see.'

'I'm doing it as fast as I can,' Inspector Cheddar grumbled.

'Hurry up. I haven't got all night.' The janitor tapped his hobnail boots on the ground.

'That's the last of them.' Inspector Cheddar rattled the final box into the cart.

'About time!' the janitor snapped.

'Shall I wheel it?' Inspector Cheddar asked generously. The janitor looked far too wizened to push it himself with all that weight in it.

'I can manage,' the janitor set off at a smart pace towards the river with the rubbish cart.

Inspector Cheddar had to run to keep up. 'Wait for me,' he puffed. The janitor really was very fit for an old-timer. He must be part of a crack team, Inspector Cheddar decided. 'I hope you don't mind me asking, but which unit are you from?' he panted.

'Er . . . the SAS.' The janitor's hobnail boots clattered on the cobbles.

'Special Air Service?' Inspector Cheddar gasped for breath.

'No – Superfit and Seventy,' the janitor explained. 'Ve're specially trained for operations like this.'

They reached the steps leading to Traitors' Gate.

'I'll take it from here,' the janitor said. He stopped the rubbish cart and reached up towards his head. 'You can have a little nap.'

'What do you mean?' Inspector Cheddar asked, bewildered. 'I don't need a little nap.' To his horror, the janitor began to peel off his bald head. Beneath it was a mat of short grey hair with sparkly bits in it. Inspector Cheddar gulped. The sparkly bits were hairpins. They twinkled in the moonlight.

'Klob!' Inspector Cheddar gasped.

'Surprise!' The janitor removed one, took aim and fired.

'Ooommpphh.' The hairpin hit Inspector Cheddar in the chest. He crumpled to the ground.

'You ninny!' Zenia Klob sniggered. 'Thinking you could trick the great Zenia Klob, mistress of disguise, with a bunch of fake Crown Jewels. Come on, Biscuit, let's get him under cover.'

A ginger head appeared from the second bin.

Between them they propped Inspector Cheddar up in a nearby sentry hut.

'That's that.' Klob clicked her boots. 'Once ve've got this lot on the barge, my murdering moggy, you can go and find Atticus and the ravens.' She winked at him. 'You know what to do.'

'Rrrrrrrrrrrr,' Ginger Biscuit bared his teeth.

'And remember, Biscuit,' Zenia Klob picked a spider off one of the cleaning brushes and offered it to him, 'Atticus has been very naughty. So don't just chew his ear this time.' She grinned as the spider's wriggling legs disappeared into Ginger Biscuit's hungry mouth. 'Chew the rest of him as vell.'

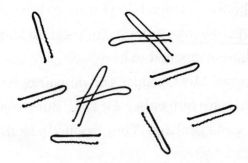

17

Mrs Cheddar, Callie and Michael were halfway to the Tube station.

Callie was crying. 'I don't want to leave Atticus,' she wept. 'He was supposed to meet us! Something must have happened to him.'

'I know!' Mrs Cheddar said despairingly. 'I don't want to leave him either. Or Dad. But we've got to go back and get help!' They trooped past the ticket office.

Michael cast a sideways glance to his right. The Tower of London loomed out of the darkness, vast and forbidding. The moat stretched round it, deep and empty. He wouldn't like to be down there right now.

Something *was* down there, though, picking its

way stealthily across the grass. Michael stopped to look more closely. He could see the dark shape of an animal heading towards the Tower walls, its white paws picked out by the moonlight. It had something square around its neck. He stopped dead.

'Isn't that Atticus?' he cried, pointing towards the moat.

Mrs Cheddar and Callie stopped too. 'Where?' Callie asked.

'I can't see anything,' Mrs Cheddar frowned.

The animal had disappeared. 'I saw him,' Michael insisted. 'I'm sure I did. He was over there, near the wall.'

'Maybe it was a shadow?' Mrs Cheddar suggested.

'No, it was him,' Michael protested. 'I saw his paws.'

'What about his red handkerchief?' Callie sniffed.

Michael shook his head. 'He wasn't wearing it. There was something else round his neck.'

Mrs Cheddar looked doubtful. 'Where could he have gone?' she asked.

'Maybe there's a tunnel!' Callie had stopped crying. Her eyes were shining with excitement. 'A secret tunnel into the castle from the moat! Maybe the ravens are safe and Atticus was trying to escape.'

'But if it really *was* Atticus Michael saw –' Mrs Cheddar frowned – 'he wasn't trying to escape; he was going back in! Why would he be doing that?'

'There's only one way to find out,' Michael said determinedly. He doubled back towards the entrance.

'Michael!' Mrs Cheddar hissed. 'What are you doing?'

'I'm going to help Atticus,' Michael called back. 'And Dad.'

'So am I.' Callie started after him.

'But what about Zenia Klob?' Mrs Cheddar cried. 'And Ginger Biscuit?'

'If the Queen isn't scared of them,' Michael said bravely, 'then neither am I.'

'Nor me,' Callie agreed.

Mrs Cheddar sighed. 'Oh well,' she said, 'I suppose I'd better come with you.'

Atticus wormed his way back through the rusty pipe from the moat to the underground bunker where the ravens were hidden. Breaking into Thumpers' Traditional Dye shop had been a piece of steak for the world's greatest ex-cat-burglar. He'd found the shop no problem and picked the lock in seconds. It was the work of a moment to grab the dye and scarper without a trace. That's not to say Atticus enjoyed doing it. He didn't. Atticus didn't want to steal any more, but he told himself that whoever owned Thumpers' would understand that it was a national emergency and that sometimes a cat burglar, even a reformed one, had to use all his powers to save Her Majesty.

The only tricky part was carrying the bottles back without his handkerchief. The stiff square carrier bag he'd found in the shop banged awkwardly against his chest. But it wasn't long before the whole operation was complete and he dropped down out of the rusty pipe back into the poo bunker.

'Waaarrrk!' The ravens were waiting for him.

Atticus pulled the bag back over his ears and took out a bottle.

The ravens crowded round.

THUMPERS'

Traditional White Beard Dye

Puts years on you in an instant.
Strongly recommended by sailors.
(Can Also Be Used on Jumpers)

'It doesn't say anything about feathers,' Georgina said doubtfully.

'Don't worry about that,' Atticus said. 'Zenia used the black one for the magpies' raven suits. And you can get it off with this.' He took out a second bottle. 'It's dye remover.'

'All right,' Georgina agreed. 'Let's do it. Come on, guys. Who's first?'

Ginger Biscuit let himself into the Bloody Tower. The hard work was over. The *real* Crown Jewels were on the barge while the fake ones were in the cabinets where the so-called electricians had put them. He chuckled. How stupid humans were (apart from Zenia, of course). And that bungling bunch pretending to be royal electricians was the most idiotic lot of humans he'd ever come across, especially the van driver. Imagine actually falling for Zenia's janitor routine! And *believing* Zenia when she told them her super-receptive hearing aid wasn't working properly! What morons. Of course it was working! He and Zenia could hear every word they whispered.

Including all the stuff about Atticus.

It hadn't taken Ginger Biscuit long to realise that the electricians were the Cheddars and that everything Jimmy Magpie said was true. Atticus Claw *was* a pet: a double-crossing, devious, lying, *spying* pet. He was a traitor. And he would pay.

Ginger Biscuit reached the room with the poo

hole. He was looking forward to this. Puncturing van tyres with his razor-sharp claws and listening to the air hiss out was fun, but not as much fun as killing ravens. As for Atticus, Ginger Biscuit hadn't yet decided whether he would finish him off in the bunker or drag him back to the barge and drown him in the mud. Atticus had never liked to do any dirty work. He always preferred to keep his precious white paws clean. The mud might be better: a more fitting end for a pampered pussycat pet.

He paced over towards the poo hole quietly. He didn't want Atticus to guess that he knew the truth. He wanted to catch him by surprise.

'Atticus?' he called softly. 'It's me, Biscuit. We've got the jewels.'

There was no reply.

'It's time to kill the ravens,' Biscuit put his head down the poo hole. The sound of his voice echoed eerily back at him.

'Killlllllll the rrrrraaaavvvveeeennnnnsssssss,' it trembled.

'If you won't do it,' Ginger Biscuit hissed, 'I will.'

'I will . . . I will . . . I will . . .' his voice whispered back.

Except it didn't sound like his voice.

Ginger Biscuit drew back sharply from the poo hole.

'Who's there?' he demanded.

'We are the ghosts of the imprisoned ravens,' the voice quivered up the poo hole and rang around the room.

'What do you mean?' Ginger Biscuit's fur began to prickle.

'We have been murdered by your accomplice, Atticus Claw,' the voice continued. 'Upon the evil order of your Gingery Biscuitness. Claw has escaped but now the Tower will fall and we will haunt you forever . . . Wooooooooooooooooooooo.'

'If that's you, Pig,' Ginger Biscuit snarled, 'you're dead.'

'It is not the one you call Pig that speaks,' the voice quavered. 'It is us, the murdered ravens of the Bloody Tower poo hole . . . waaaaarrrrrrrkkkkk!'

'I don't believe you,' Ginger Biscuit began to tremble all over. 'You're not really ghosts. You're making it up.'

'Then we will show ourselves to you,' the voice breathed.

'No!' Ginger Biscuit's fur stood on end. 'There's no need. Really. I'm leaving anyway. If you're dead the whole place will collapse.'

'The White Tower will be the first to fall,' the hollow voice cried. 'And once the axe man, the wailing woman, and our poor headless friend Anne Boleyn find out what you have done, I wouldn't like to be in your paws.'

'But I didn't do anything!' Ginger Biscuit howled. 'It was Claw.'

'It was you who gave the order. It is you who face the terrible curse.' The voice was relentless. 'We are coming . . .'

There was a soft fluttering sound.

Ginger Biscuit stared in horror. Six white birds emerged from the poo hole one after another. FLAP. FLAP. FLAP. FLAP. FLAP. FLAP. They hovered in the air in front of him.

The biggest one stared at him with huge black eyes. 'There can be no escape . . .' The birds lurched towards him.

With a yowl of terror, Ginger Biscuit turned

and ran.

'Waaarrrk! Waaarrrk! Waaarrrk!'

'Waaarrrk! Waaarrrk! Waaarrrk!'

The six ravens collapsed to the floor, laughing.

'Nice work, guys!' Georgina congratulated the others. 'I haven't done that much flying in ages! Now let's get Atticus.' They hopped over to the curtains, unhooked the rope ties and twisted them together in a tight knot. Then they settled back beside the poo hole. 'Are you ready?' Georgina called down.

'I'm ready,' Atticus's voice echoed up the shaft. 'Nice haunting, by the way. I wish I could have seen Biscuit's face.'

'He was completely spooked,' Georgina chuckled. 'Come on, guys. Heave-ho.' She took hold of one end of the curtain rope in her powerful beak and pushed the other end over the edge of the shaft. The other ravens followed suit. The rope went taut. They braced themselves.

Down below, in the bunker, Atticus grabbed the rope. Slowly, inch by inch, he hauled himself up the shaft.

'Phew!' he said, collapsing on to the floor.

Atticus pulled the stiff Thumpers' bag from around his neck. 'Sorry if I was a bit heavier than you expected. But I thought you might want this.' It was the bottle of Thumpers' Dye Remover.

'Thanks, Atticus,' Georgina pulled the stopper out with her beak. 'What should we do when we're back to black?'

'Go to the raven pens and hide out in the hut until Ron gets back,' Atticus told her. 'That's the last place Klob would look. Anyway,' he added, 'she thinks you're dead.'

He headed towards the spiral staircase.

'Where are you going?' Georgina asked.

Atticus grinned. 'I'm going to find my family.'

18

'Chaka-chaka-chaka-chaka-chaka!'

On the barge, the magpies chattered and squawked. Zenia was on deck fitting the latest Russian turbo-engine ready for their getaway. Ginger Biscuit was out killing ravens and Atticus. It was their turn to have a bit of fun.

'Well,' Thug said. '*Does* it suit me?' The magpies had flicked open the plastic toolboxes to look at the treasure. Pig, Wally and Gizzard were lying in a bath of rings and orbs. Jimmy was checking out the crowns and Thug and Slasher were snuggling under the ermine coronation gown.

'It looks lovely with the blue of your wings,' Slasher told him.

'It's so soft!' Thug rubbed his cheek against the

fur. 'It would make a perfect nest snuggler. 'Ere, Jimmy, can you knit one of these?'

'*King* Jimmy, you mean!' Jimmy's voice came from beneath the crown. 'I could do with something like this in Littleton-on-Sea. It'd be good for my image.'

'Yeah, real good, Boss,' Pig agreed. 'Very regal.'

Just then Ginger Biscuit raced in, his tail between his legs.

The magpies stared at him.

'What's up with you?' Wally said.

'You look like you've seen a ghost!' Thug sniggered.

'I have!' Ginger Biscuit yelped. 'Not just one ghost! Six of them.'

'What?' Jimmy pushed the crown off and hopped on to the table.

'The ravens!' Ginger Biscuit let out a strangled cry. 'Claw killed them.'

'That's what you told him to do,' Wally said, 'wasn't it?'

'Not until I gave him the word,' Ginger Biscuit yowled. 'He's gone and done it on his own and now they're after me!'

'You sure?' Slasher asked.

'Yes.' Ginger Biscuit closed his eyes. 'They flew out of the poo hole; all white and creepy.' He shuddered. 'They say I'm responsible. They say I'm cursed!' He began to dip hairpins into the bottle of sleeping potion to take his mind off things.

'Hang on a minute,' Thug scratched his bottom. 'If the ravens are dead, then why hasn't the White Tower fallen? People should be revolting.'

'What, like Wally?' Slasher joked.

'Chaka-chaka-chaka-chaka-chaka!'

'Maybe it takes a while,' Ginger Biscuit said miserably. 'I don't know. We should probably get out of here while we still can. Wait a minute!' he snarled. 'This isn't sleeping potion.' The tip of the silver hairpins had turned black. 'It's that dye Zenia used on the raven suits.'

'Dye!' Jimmy repeated, his voice sharp. 'I wonder . . .' He eyed the bottle. 'Atticus Claw knows all about dye.'

'What do you mean?' Ginger Biscuit froze.

'He dyed himself white to fool us when we did the Toffly Hall job,' Jimmy told him. 'He pretended he was a Persian cat so we wouldn't notice him sneak in.' Jimmy put his head to one side, thinking. 'Where's the dye shop?' he said suddenly.

'55 Tower Vaults,' Slasher read the label.

'That's the other side of the moat.' Jimmy's eyes glittered. 'Is there any chance Claw could have got his paws on some?'

'You can get to the moat from the poo hole.' Ginger Biscuit frowned. 'There's a pipe.'

'Did Claw know about it?' Jimmy asked sharply.

Ginger Biscuit nodded. 'I told him.'

'That's it, then.' Jimmy shrugged. 'What could be easier for a measly ex-burglar like Atticus Claw than to nip to Thumpers', steal a bottle of white dye and cover the ravens with it?'

'But . . .'

'Put it this way, Ginger,' Jimmy interrupted, 'the White Tower hasn't fallen. The Queen's still on the throne. And Slasher's right: the only revolting thing around here is Wally. You didn't see any ghosts. What you saw was a bunch of ravens covered in Thumpers' Traditional White. I don't like to say I told you so, but I did. Atticus Claw is a low-down double-crossing liar. He's tricked you. *Again*.'

There was silence in the cabin. The six magpies

had their eyes glued on Ginger Biscuit.

'Uh-oh,' said Thug. 'He looks like he's about to lay an egg.'

'MMMMYYYYYYAAAAAAAWWWWWW!' All of a sudden Ginger Biscuit went bananas. He smashed the bottle of feather dye. He ripped the sofa. He puffed himself up to twice his normal size and flung the bowl of hairpins to the floor. Finally he scraped his claws along the wooden table, showering the magpies with sharp splinters. His face contorted into a hideous snarl. 'THAT . . . CAT . . . IS . . . DEAD!' He hurtled out of the barge in a flash of ginger, breaking the door off its hinges, and disappeared into the night.

'What's that?'

Mrs Cheddar, Callie and Michael were searching the Tower for Atticus and Inspector Cheddar.

'It sounds like a werewolf,' Michael said, staring at the full moon.

'A were-cat more like,' Mrs Cheddar muttered.

'I hope Atticus is all right,' Callie was gulped.

'Shhhh!' Mrs Cheddar pulled the children into

the shadows.

Ginger Biscuit bounded past them, snarling.

'Do you think he's found out about Atticus?' Michael asked.

'From the look on his face, I think he must have,' Mrs Cheddar shivered. 'We need to find Atticus before he does.'

'And Dad,' Callie sniffed.

'Oooohhhhhhhh.'

The groaning noise came from nearby.

Mrs Cheddar, Callie and Michael froze.

'It's probably just the wind,' Mrs Cheddar said nervously.

'Oooooohhhhhhh.'

'It's not windy.' Michael's face was white.

'Oooooooooohhhhhhhhhhhh.'

The three terrified Cheddars turned around slowly.

'DAD!' Callie cried.

Inspector Cheddar fell out of the sentry hut on to the ground.

Mrs Cheddar dropped to her knees. 'He's been hairpinned,' she said grimly. She put her lips to her husband's ear. 'Don't move, darling.'

'I'm fine,' Inspector Cheddar tried to sit up. 'Just a bit groggy.' He rubbed his forehead. 'Where's that witch, Klob?'

'We don't know, Dad,' Michael told him. 'Where are the real Crown Jewels?'

'Klob's got them,' Inspector Cheddar said in a slurred voice. 'She pretended to be a janitor. She told me the Queen sent her.' He propped himself up on one elbow. 'She was taking them to the river. She must be loading them on to a boat.'

'The barge!' Michael said suddenly. 'I'll bet that's where she's been holed up.'

'Of course!' Mrs Cheddar exclaimed.

Inspector Cheddar propped himself up on the other elbow. 'We've got to stop her before she gets to the airport.'

'I reckon she's still here, Dad,' Michael said. 'We just saw Biscuit. She wouldn't leave without him.'

'What about the ravens?' Inspector Cheddar staggered to his feet.

'We don't know where they are but they must be safe,' Mrs Cheddar said. 'Thanks to Atticus.'

'Where *is* Atticus?' Inspector Cheddar peered into the darkness, swaying slightly. 'Did you find him?'

'No!' Callie said despairingly. 'We think Ginger Biscuit's looking for him. He went past a few minutes ago, hissing and spitting like mad.'

'He'll kill Atticus if he's found out he's a spy!' Michael cried. 'Come on, Dad. We've got to *do* something to help him.'

Inspector Cheddar straightened his electrician's cap. 'I'm not letting any cat of Klob's kill one of my officers,' he said firmly. 'Which way did he go?'

Atticus doubled back across the courtyard to make sure the Cheddars weren't still waiting for him at the Jewel House. He stopped dead when he saw the broken-down van. *Where were they? And what had happened to the Crown Jewels?!*

'MMMMYYYYYYAAAAAAAWWWWWWW!'

Atticus's fur stood on end. It was Ginger Biscuit. *He knew!*

Atticus didn't have time to wonder *how* Ginger Biscuit knew. His first thought was for the safety of the ravens. His second was for himself. And, thinking about it a bit more carefully, he decided, it should have been the other way around. Ginger Biscuit had forgotten about the ravens. All Biscuit cared about now was revenge.

Atticus retraced his steps across the courtyard, keeping to the shadows. The quickest way out was back through the archway past the Bloody Tower, but that might be the first place Biscuit would look. He needed to be careful. He'd got halfway when he heard a voice calling his name.

'Atticus!'

Atticus could hardly believe his ears. It was Michael!

'Atticus!'

And Callie!

'Atticus!'

And Inspector and Mrs Cheddar!

Atticus's heart glowed. The Cheddars had waited for him. They were trying to find him, before Biscuit did. He bounded towards the voices.

'There he is!'

The Cheddars had reached Tower Green. They started running towards him.

Atticus leapt into Callie's arms.

'Oh, Atticus, we're so pleased to see you!' Callie buried her face in his fur.

'We were so worried about you!' Michael scratched his ears.

'We thought that horrible ginger cat might have got to you first!' Mrs Cheddar held his paw.

'Well done for keeping the ravens safe!' Inspector Cheddar tickled his tummy. 'It was a brilliant bit of police-catting.'

Atticus purred throatily.

'MMYYYYYYYYAAAAAAWWWWWWWW!'

Atticus's blood went cold.

The Cheddar family turned.

Ginger Biscuit was advancing towards them from the direction of the Bloody Tower, his ears flat to his head.

'I'll handle this.' Inspector Cheddar took a step towards Biscuit and put his hand up as though he was stopping traffic. 'Hold it right there,' he ordered.

Atticus swallowed. He didn't think this was a good idea. Inspector Cheddar didn't realise what Ginger Biscuit was capable of.

Ginger Biscuit kept on coming.

'Darling . . .' Mrs Cheddar began.

Inspector Cheddar shook his head. 'Not now.' He held up his other hand. 'I said, stop,' he commanded.

Ginger Biscuit ignored him. He slithered along on his belly, his pale blue eyes fixed on Atticus.

Atticus shook with fear. Inspector Cheddar was no match for Ginger Biscuit.

'All right, Biscuit, if it's trouble you want . . .' Inspector Cheddar took a pair of handcuffs out of his overall pocket and held them up. 'Try these for size.'

Ginger Biscuit seemed to notice Inspector Cheddar for the first time. He stopped and regarded him with a hostile stare. '*SSSSSSSSSSSSSS.*'

'That's more like it,' Inspector Cheddar took another step towards him. 'It may come as a surprise to you, Biscuit, but I'm not really a royal electrician. I'm an officer of the law.'

Atticus clung on to Callie, terrified.

'*SSSSSSSSSSSSS.*'

'And I'm arresting you on suspicion of stealing the Crown Jewels.' Inspector Cheddar made a lunge for Biscuit. 'You do not have to meow any-

thing, but anything you do meow may be taken down and used as evidence against you in a court of law.'

There was a flash of ginger.

'AARRRRGGGGHHHH!' Inspector Cheddar lay spreadeagled on the ground. Ginger Biscuit was on his back. SNAP! There was a sound of metal on metal. 'The beastly Biscuit's handcuffed me!'

Ginger Biscuit jumped away, snarling, the key to the handcuffs between his teeth. He tossed it out of reach.

'SSSSSSSSSSSSS!' Biscuit glanced at Atticus. Then his pale blue eyes turned on Michael and Callie. POP. POP. POP. POP. One by one he popped out the claws on his right forepaw. POP. POP. POP. POP. Then on his left.

Atticus watched, horrified.

'Don't be frightened, kids,' Mrs Cheddar stepped in front of them. Her voice trembled. 'Everything will be all right.'

At that moment Atticus knew he loved the Cheddars more than anything else in the whole world. He also knew that everything *wouldn't* be

all right unless he acted fast. Biscuit was the world's meanest cat. And he was after one thing and one thing only: *HIM!* Ginger Biscuit didn't care who got hurt in the process: even women and children weren't safe when he was around. There was only one thing to do. Atticus gave a quick wriggle and jumped out of Callie's arms.

'Atticus!'

Ignoring the Cheddars' cries, he flew past Ginger Biscuit.

Ginger Biscuit was taken by surprise. 'MMYYYA-AAWWWWWW!' With a roar of anger he turned and raced after Atticus.

20

Atticus dodged past the Bloody Tower, through the archway and back on to the cobbled street. He skidded to a halt. Ahead of him was Traitors' Gate. For a moment he thought of charging down the steps and along the muddy bank, hiding in the murky shallows away from the barge. Biscuit wouldn't think to look for him down there; he knew Atticus hated mud. But then Atticus heard the water slapping at the stone. The tide was in. There was no escape that way. Only a gloopy, sticky death.

He glanced to his right, towards the portcullis and the bridge over the moat. Atticus gulped. Zenia Klob was standing a few feet away from him. *Zip!* A hairpin winged past his whiskers. It clinked as it hit the ground. He saw Zenia raise her hand to her head. She was getting ready to fire another one. This time she wouldn't miss. He'd have to find a different way out.

'MMYYAAAWWWWW!' Behind him, Ginger Biscuit was closing fast.

Atticus sprinted to his left. Ahead of him he could see Tower Bridge, lit up against the night sky. If only he could get on to it, then he could chase back towards the Tube station and get help, or dash across to the other side of the river where the Commissioner had some of his officers posted. It didn't really matter which way he went. Ginger Biscuit would follow him. And as long as Biscuit was following him, he couldn't hurt the Cheddars, or the ravens, or the Queen.

There was an opening to his right. Atticus took it. All of a sudden he found himself on a walkway suspended above the Thames. Atticus turned left and charged towards Tower Bridge.

'MMYYAAAWWWW!' Ginger Biscuit wasn't far behind.

Atticus raced on. His legs were aching. The problem with being a pet was that you didn't get as much exercise as you did when you were a cat burglar. If he ever got back to Littleton-on-Sea he'd have to do something about that. Maybe he and Mimi could go on some walks together. But he mustn't think about Mimi now. Panting hard, he reached the end of the walkway and started up the steep steps to the bridge. He didn't turn around. Ginger Biscuit was gaining on him. The ginger cat's cries were growing louder: they echoed savagely in Atticus's ears.

'MMYYAAAWWWW!'

Atticus clambered up. The steps seemed to go on forever. His heart was hammering. His paws were sore. *Keep going,* he urged himself. *The further away Ginger Biscuit is from the Cheddars and the ravens, the better.* He struggled up the last few steps.

'SSSSSSSSSSSS!' Ginger Biscuit was seconds behind. 'You're for it, Claw.'

Atticus looked about wildly, trying to decide which way to go. He didn't know the way to the Tube from here! But he didn't know how to find the Commissioner's men on the other side of the river either! He took a few steps along the bridge.

'Any last words?' Ginger Biscuit had reached the bridge. Atticus backed away. He didn't have a choice now. He had to cross Tower Bridge. Exhausted, he stumbled towards the other side. It was hard going – like climbing a hill. It seemed to get steeper and steeper. Atticus crept on. He was so tired he could barely put one paw in front of another. He glanced behind. Ginger Biscuit had slowed down too, crawling up the slope behind him, like a lion ready to pounce, his pale blue eyes fixed on Atticus. Atticus shook his head. Something was wrong. The bridge *was* getting steeper and steeper! He *wasn't* just imagining it. What was going on?

'CHAKA-CHAKA-CHAKA-CHAKA-CHAKA!'

Atticus looked up. Five magpies were circling above him, chattering with laughter.

'Try to steal my ermine, would you?' Thug taunted.

'Double-crossing cat!' Slasher cawed.

'Biscuit's going to crunch you,' Pig grunted.

'What's happening?' Atticus demanded, trying to keep his voice strong. He felt himself slipping

backwards, towards Ginger Biscuit. He gripped on with his claws and hauled himself forwards.

'This is better than teasing robins!' Gizzard chuckled.

'It's almost as good as pooing on washing!' Wally agreed.

The magpies flapped and chattered.

> 'Atticus Claw is falling down,
> Falling down,
> Falling down,
> Atticus Claw is falling down,
> 'Cos of the magpies.'

'Tell me what's going on!' Atticus wanted to pin them but he couldn't. He needed both front paws to hang on.

'I thought you'd have guessed by now,' Slasher crowed.

'Yeah, not so smart now, are you, Atticus Claw,' Thug cawed.

'Jimmy's in the control tower,' Gizzard explained.

'He's opening the bridge,' Pig laughed.

'You've had it, pussycat!' Wally hooted.

Atticus twisted his head. Above him at a high window he could just make out the silhouette of Jimmy Magpie. He had a lever in his beak. Now Atticus understood. He'd seen pictures of Tower Bridge in Mrs Cheddar's guidebook. It opened in the middle to let ships through – the two sides lifting vertically up in the air. That was what was happening now. That was why he felt like he was climbing a mountain. He was!

'Give up yet, Claw?'

Atticus felt sharp claws reach for his tail. He twitched it away, just in time. 'Never!' he hissed, clinging on to the top of the bridge.

'I should have killed you when I had the chance the last time,' Ginger Biscuit was so close Atticus could smell his ratty breath. 'You couldn't finish the job then and you couldn't finish it now. I should have known you'd never have the guts to kill those ravens.'

'I don't like killing,' Atticus said. He was going to die anyway. He might as well tell Biscuit the truth. 'I won't do it. Not for you. Or Klob. Or anyone. The ravens are safe thanks to me. And I'm proud of it.'

'It doesn't make any difference,' Ginger Biscuit snapped furiously. 'Zenia and I got what we came for – the real Crown Jewels. Your stupid Cheddar family couldn't fool us with their dumb electricians' disguises. Zenia got them off the Inspector, no problem. They're on the barge.'

This was news to Atticus. But it didn't matter about the Crown Jewels. The ravens were safe. So were the Cheddars. And the monarchy. Atticus had a feeling that Her Majesty would be pleased.

'People are more important than jewels, Biscuit,' Atticus whispered. 'So is friendship and loyalty. That's something you'll never understand.'

There was a flash of ginger. *FLIP!* All of a sudden Atticus found himself dangling by his claws over the edge of the open bridge. Biscuit was sitting above him, perfectly balanced. He seemed to have no fear. Atticus glanced down. The river was miles beneath, the water twinkling in the moonlight. A little way along the bank he could see Klob's barge floating towards them. There was only one other boat on the river. It was moving swiftly along in the opposite direction. He wondered vaguely if the Commissioner was on it. Or Monica Mint. Or the Queen. It didn't matter. It was too late for him. Atticus felt sick. His head was swimming. His claws ached.

'Don't lecture me about loyalty, Claw.' Biscuit's face loomed above him. The magpies were flapping about his head. 'It won't make any difference where you're going.' POP. POP. POP. POP. 'Goodbye . . .' Ginger Biscuit reached for Atticus's throat. '. . . loser.' He shoved him off the bridge.

'CHAKA-CHAKA-CHAKA-CHAKA-CHAKA!'

The last thing Atticus saw was Jimmy Magpie, swooping towards him with wild, glittering eyes.

21.

Atticus felt himself falling . . . falling . . . falling. The air rippled his fur. Any minute now and he would feel the water coming up to meet him like an iced brick. His life flashed before him – his kittenhood with Ginger Biscuit and Klob; his escape to Monte Carlo; the international life of cat-burgling that followed; the magpies; his home with the Cheddars; Mrs Tucker's basket of fresh sardines . . . He heard a roar and closed his eyes.

THWUMP! He landed in something soft. The roar subsided.

PUTT-PUTT-PUTT-PUTT-PUTT-PUTT. It was replaced by a chugging noise.

Atticus sniffed. He could smell fish. Without opening his eyes he put out a paw. Whatever he had landed on was woolly and hairy; all knitted together in a big tangle. There were bits in it too. Tentatively he picked one out with a claw and put it in his mouth. A morsel of sardine! Atticus felt a growing excitement. *It couldn't be! Could it?*

'Youze all right in there, Atticus?' A man's voice boomed in one ear.

'We got here as fast as we could.' A woman's voice bellowed in the other. 'Just as well by the looks of things,' it added disapprovingly. 'Falling off bridges when we've paid for you to be having a nice quiet holiday – you can't take some cats anywhere!'

'Meow!' Atticus cried joyfully. He opened both eyes. He could hardly believe his luck. He had landed in Mr Tucker's beard-jumper! Mrs Tucker was there too. The two of them were standing on something solid*ish* in the middle of the Thames, rocking gently to and fro, with their hands on their hips, staring at him.

'Edna thought you might need a little help,' Mr Tucker chuckled, lifting him gently off his beard-jumper and sitting him on a pile of nets. 'So we

188

dropped everything and jumped in me old rust-bucket of a fishing boat and sailed here as quickly as we could!' He shivered. 'I thought we was too late for a minute when I saw youze hanging off the edge there. It's lucky we made it.'

'Meow?' Atticus was puzzled. *How did they know he was in trouble?*

'I expect you're wondering how we knew you were in trouble.' Mrs Tucker glared at him. 'Apart from the fact that you're the sort of cat who's always in trouble!'

Atticus's chewed ear drooped.

'Don't youze worry, Atticus,' Mr Tucker whispered. 'She doesn't really mean it. I've never seen her so worried.'

'Fortunately for you,' Mrs Tucker continued crossly, 'we saw Klob's broadcast. So I picked up the hotline to the Prime Minister. He told me you'd been to see the Queen and let me in on her plan.'

Atticus stared at her. His whiskers twitched. *Mrs Tucker? Phoning the Prime Minister?? On the hotline???*

'There's no need to look so surprised, Atticus,' Mrs Tucker snapped. 'I haven't spent my whole life cleaning fishhooks and gutting sardines. Before I married Mr Tucker I was Edna Whelk, secret agent.'

Atticus's mouth dropped open. *Mrs Tucker a secret agent?*

'Here.' Mrs Tucker reached into her basket and shoved a sardine between his teeth. 'In those days I worked for MI6. My mission was to capture Klob.' Mrs Tucker's eyes narrowed. 'I came close a couple of times, but she always gave me the slip with those disguises of hers, not to mention a couple of hairpins in the backside.'

'The Prime Minister thought if youze were working on the case for Her Majesty, Atticus,' Mr Tucker said, 'Edna might like another crack at catching Klob.' He lit his pipe and sucked on it noisily.

'Darned right, I would!' Mrs Tucker exclaimed. 'I'd have nailed her by now if *someone –*' she waggled her finger at Atticus – 'had bothered to tell me what was going on sooner. *And* I'd have bagged those mangy magpies. *And* that beastly ginger cat, Digestive Biscuit, or whatever his name is. Anyway, better late than never, I suppose.' She rolled up her

sleeves. 'Get me the night-vision binoculars, Herman,' she ordered. 'And be quick about it.'

Mr Tucker clanked across the deck. 'Blaaaarrrrst this wooden leg,' he cursed. 'It makes me slower than a sea slug with scabies.' He clanked back with the binoculars.

'Pass them here.' Mrs Tucker grabbed them.

'What can you see, Edna?' Mr Tucker asked anxiously, cutting the engine and letting the boat idle. 'Any sea monsters?'

'Don't be silly, Herman, this is the River Thames, not the Pacific Ocean.' She twiddled the focus. 'Biscuit's coming down the steps from Tower Bridge. He's on the walkway. He's waiting for something.'

The barge! Atticus thought.

'Hold on . . .' Mrs Tucker adjusted the binoculars. 'There's a barge pulling alongside. Biscuit's walking towards it. He's jumping on board. The magpies are following him.'

'Can you see Klob?' Mr Tucker demanded.

'There's someone at the helm.' Mrs Tucker sucked in a big gulp of air. 'It's her all right: I can see the hairpins.'

Atticus followed her gaze. He didn't need night-vision binoculars. Cats can see in the dark and it was easy for him to make out the barge and the figures on board.

The barge pulled away. Mrs Tucker tucked the binoculars under her armpit. 'Right. Here's the plan. We'll give Klob a head start so she doesn't suspect anything. Then we'll ram the barge and board it. I'll take Klob. Herman and Atticus – you net Biscuit and the magpies.' She rubbed her backside. 'And watch out for hairpins.'

Mr Tucker nodded. 'Aye aye, Agent Whelk!'

Atticus jumped off the nets. Four more figures had appeared on the walkway.

'Meow!' he yowled. 'Meow! Meow! Meow!'

'It's the Cheddars!' Mrs Tucker held the binoculars up again. 'Quick, Herman. Let's pick them up. We could do with some extra help.'

The boat chugged quietly towards the walkway.

'Ahoy there, mateys!' Mr Tucker pulled alongside.

'It's Mr Tucker!' Michael cried.

'And Mrs Tucker!' Mrs Cheddar waved.

'And Atticus!' Callie yelled 'He's all right!'

'What are you two doing here?' Inspector Cheddar asked, bewildered.

'No time to explain now,' Mrs Tucker said quickly. 'We're after Klob. She's getting away. We need to hurry.'

'You three go,' Inspector Cheddar said. 'I'll meet you at the airport, just in case you don't catch her. I need to warn the Commissioner that she's got the real Crown Jewels.'

'Don't tell me you fell for her old janitor routine?' Mrs Tucker sounded exasperated.

'How did you know about her old janitor routine?' Inspector Cheddar gawped at her.

'Never mind,' Mrs Tucker said. 'Let's go.'

Callie, Michael and Mrs Cheddar jumped on to the boat.

'Put these on,' Mrs Tucker ordered. She handed them three life vests.

THE JOLLY JELLYFISH. The boat's name was written on them.

'Is this the boat you've had all the adventures in, Mr Tucker?' Callie asked, putting the life vest over her head and velcroing the straps. 'The one that got attacked by the giant lobster?'

'Aye!' Mr Tucker flicked his false teeth in and out with a rattle. 'Youze can trust *The Jolly Jellyfish* with your life. She be a fisherman's friend.' He started tapping his wooden leg on the deck to get a rhythm going.

Atticus knew what was coming: Mr Tucker had a habit of breaking into sea shanties when he was on an adventure.

'Don't youze worry if youze hit a rock,
Me ship's as safe as a salmon in a sock . . .
She may be a tub but she's still me boat,
She can sail through a hurricane and stay afloat.'

Michael and Callie were giggling. Atticus found his whiskers twitching along in time with the song.

'When the giant lobster chewed me leg off at sea,
All the blood gurgled out and I felt ropey,
Luckily I plugged it with me jumper-beard,
And me and the Jellyfish sailed back unafeared.'

'Shut up, Herman,' Mrs Tucker hissed. 'You'll make everyone seasick.'

They waved goodbye to Inspector Cheddar and *The Jolly Jellyfish* glided silently out into the water.

22

PUTT-PUTT-PUTT-PUTT-PUTT-PUTT.

'What's that?' On board the barge, Zenia Klob had just switched on her super-receptive hearing aid, ready to intercept any signals from the Commissioner in case the police gave chase before she got to the airport and made her getaway to Siberia.

Ginger Biscuit pricked up his ears.

'Ve're being followed,' Zenia Klob whispered. She upped the volume on the hearing aid and frowned. 'By a fisherman vith one leg, a set of false teeth and a beard-jumper in a boat called *The Jolly Jellyfish* . . .' She shrugged. 'If that's the best they've got ve're home and dry.'

PUTT-PUTT-PUTT-PUTT-PUTT-PUTT.

'Myaaawwww!' Ginger Biscuit pointed to the stern.

'Chaka-chaka-chaka-chaka-chaka!' The magpies began to chatter.

'Shut up!' Zenia Klob ordered. 'Or I'll put you in a pie.'

The magpies fell silent.

PUTT-PUTT-PUTT-PUTT-PUTT-PUTT.

The Jolly Jellyfish came into view. The fisherman was at the tiller, puffing away at a pipe. He waved.

Zenia Klob gave him an evil stare.

'Time to give our fishy friend a taste of the latest Russian turbo-technology, Biscuit.' Zenia Klob grinned. 'Don't you agree?'

'Myaaaawwww,' Ginger Biscuit bared his teeth.

'Hold on to your feathers, birdies,' Zenia screeched at the magpies. 'You're in for a bumpy ride.' She reached over the back of the barge and pulled a lever.

WHOOSHHHHHHHHHHHHH!

The barge sprang forwards. 'Vorp speed ahead!' Zenia cackled.

'Chaka-chaka-chaka-chaka-chaka!'

The magpies hung on grimly to the rail. Their

feathers flapped and rippled.

'SSSSSSSSSSSSSSS!'

Ginger Biscuit hung on too. His whiskers were pushed flat against his cheeks.

'Ha-ha!' Zenia Klob shrieked. 'Ve're losing them.'

VVVVRRRROOOOOOMMMMMMM!

The Jolly Jellyfish came back into view. The fisherman gave them another wave.

'I don't believe it!' Zenia Klob screamed. 'They're gaining on us!' She pushed the lever to MAX. The barge charged ahead.

'Chakchakchakchakhakchakchakchakchak!' The magpies juddered about, their eyes popping.

'SSSSSSSSSSSSSS!'

Ginger Biscuit's tail streamed out behind him like a rudder.

ZZZOOOOOOMMMMMMMMMM!

The Jolly Jellyfish was back again. The fisherman gave a thumbs-up signal.

'They're going to ram us!' Zenia Klob cried.

The Jolly Jellyfish roared alongside the barge. 'Surprise!' a voice shouted. A stout figure emerged from the cabin wearing an enormous pair of rubber waders and a big yellow hat. She stood beside the fisherman.

Zenia Klob stared in disbelief. 'Agent Velk!' she gasped.

'You got it,' Mrs Tucker shouted. 'Now give yourself up, Klob, or I'll come and get you.'

'Never!' Zenia Klob reached for the lever. She pushed it to EXTRA MAX. The barge sped off.

'Chakchakchakchakchakchakchak!'

'SSSSSSSSSSSSS!'

WWHIIIIIIZZZZZZ!

The Jolly Jellyfish zoomed up. Mr Tucker gave Zenia another wave.

'You can't outrun us, Klob,' Mrs Tucker yelled. 'We're faster than you.'

'I don't believe it!' Zenia Klob burst out. 'How did *you* get hold of the latest Russian turbo-technology? It's top secret.'

'We didn't,' Mr Tucker shouted. 'Me engine runs on bottled shaaarrrrk faaaarrrrt. It's the faaarrrstest fish fuel in the ocean.'

'Face it, Klob. The game's up!' Mrs Tucker bawled. 'You can't escape this time.'

'Wanna bet?' Zenia Klob yanked the lever to

EXTRA DANGER MAX.

'Chakchakchakchakchakchak!'

'SSSSSSSSSSSSSSSS!'

BOOM!

There was a loud explosion. The barge came to a shuddering halt in a cloud of smoke.

'Bring us alongside, Herman!' Mrs Tucker yelled.

PUTT-PUTT-PUTT-PUTT-PUTT-PUTT.

Mr Tucker manoeuvred *The Jolly Jellyfish* so that it was right next to the barge. He fastened the two boats together with a thick rope.

'Get the nets!'

Michael, Callie and Mrs Cheddar grabbed the pile of folded nets.

'I'm going on.' Mrs Tucker clambered across the rail of the sailing boat on to the front of the barge. 'Yoo-hoo, Klob-face! Over here!'

Atticus jumped nimbly after her. He tiptoed along the deck and hid behind a plant pot. He didn't want Biscuit to see him yet. He had a feeling he might be needed later.

At the other end of the boat, Ginger Biscuit was wiping the smoke out of his eyes.

'Chaka-chaka-chaka-chaka-chaka-chaka-chaka!' The magpies coughed and spluttered.

'Vait there, vile I fix Velk.' Zenia Klob moved off down the barge.

Callie and Mrs Cheddar took hold of one end of the net. Mr Tucker and Michael grabbed the other.

'Ready, Cheddars?' Mr Tucker yelled.

'Ready!' They shouted back.

SWOOOSSSH! They threw the net across the barge.

Ginger Biscuit leapt for safety. The magpies looked up in alarm.

FLOP! The net descended on the magpies.

'Got youze!' Mr Tucker yelled.

'Chaka-chaka-chaka-chaka-chaka!' The magpies flapped and hopped and chattered.

'Not again!' Thug moaned.

'It's just like the bloomin' Toffly Hall fiasco!' Slasher grumbled.

'Biscuit!' Jimmy squawked. 'Get us out of here.'

SCHWIPPP! There was a flash of ginger fur.

'Ladies first,' Ginger Biscuit opened the hole in the net where his claws had sliced through the tough nylon.

200

'Thanks very much!' Thug hopped out.

'Chaka-chaka-chaka-chaka-chaka!' The other magpies struggled free.

'He's ripped me best barracuda net!' Mr Tucker shouted. 'The beast!'

Atticus watched from behind the plant pot. He wasn't surprised. Ginger Biscuit's claws were sharper than butchers' knives.

'What do we do now?' Mrs Cheddar asked.

Mr Tucker rolled up his sleeves. 'No one rips me best barracuda net and gets away with it.' He began to climb across on to the barge.

23

'We'd better go with him,' Michael said. 'In case he gets his wooden leg stuck.'

The Cheddars clambered across too.

'Hurry up, Herman!' At the other end of the barge Mrs Tucker was locked in battle with Zenia Klob.

Atticus peeked out from his hiding place. Mrs Tucker was pelting Zenia with sardines. They were hidden in the pockets of her rubber trousers!

SPLAT! 'Take that, Klob!' The first wave hit Zenia in the eye.

SPLAT! SPLAT! The second wave took out her super-receptive hearing aid.

SPLAT! SPLAT! SPLAT! The third wave left a trail of scales across her chin.

Zip! Zip! Zip! Zenia retaliated with a barrage of hairpins. 'Get over here, Biscuit!' she screeched. 'I could do vith a little help.'

Atticus tried to think what to do. So far, Mrs Tucker's enormous rubber trousers and large waterproof hat had stopped Zenia's hairpins. But with Ginger Biscuit on the loose that wouldn't last for long. Biscuit had claws that could chop wood. He would slice through a bit of yellow rubber in no time.

'*SSSSSSSSSSS!*'

'What are you doing, Herman?' Mrs Tucker yelled. 'You're supposed to be catching the Digestive Biscuit.'

'Me leg's stuck faster than a barnacle on a bilge pump!' Mr Tucker roared. 'Come on, kids. Heave!'

Callie and Michael had made it on to the barge with Mrs Cheddar. They took hold of Mr Tucker's hairy hands and pulled.

SLAP! Zip! SLAP! Zip! SLAP! Mrs Tucker and Zenia fought on.

POP. POP. POP. POP. Ginger Biscuit got ready to rip rubber.

'Chaka-chaka-chaka-chaka-chaka!' The magpies

were all chattering at once.

Atticus sighed. *Here we go again!* he thought.

He stepped out from his hiding place.

'Over here, Biscuit!'

Ginger Biscuit turned. 'Claw?' he whispered. 'It can't be. I saw you fall off the bridge. You're dead.'

'Uh-uh.' Atticus shook his head. 'You forgot something, Biscuit. Cats have nine lives. I had eight left after the last time you tried to kill me. I've still got seven.'

'RRRRRRRRRRR,' Ginger Biscuit took a step towards him.

'Over here, Atticus,' Mr Tucker called. 'Cheddars, get in the cabin where it's safe. Check the Crown Jewels are there. I'll unscrew me leg and pull it out meself.'

The children and Mrs Cheddar hurried below.

Atticus retreated towards Mr Tucker.

Ginger Biscuit advanced, his belly to the deck.

'I'm nearly out of sardines!' Mrs Tucker shouted desperately. 'Mayday! Mayday!'

'Say goodbye, Claw,' Ginger Biscuit said. He puffed up his orange fur.

'Leave him to me, Atticus!'

Atticus looked up. Mr Tucker stood beside him swaying dangerously. In one hand he held his wooden leg.

Ginger Biscuit looked from one to the other, deciding what to do. 'I'll take out the old-timer first,' he boasted, 'then I'll get you.' There was a flash of ginger.

Mr Tucker swiped at Biscuit with his wooden leg and missed. 'Darn it!' he yelled, falling over. 'He's in me beard-jumper!'

Atticus stared. Ginger Biscuit's studded collar had got stuck in the tangle!

SCHWIPP! Ginger Biscuit tried to hack his way out. Bits of beard-jumper flew about the deck. *SCHWIPP! SCHWIPP! SCHWIPP-SCHWIPP-SCHWIPP!* The more he struggled the more tangled he got. 'Help me, you stupid magpies!' he roared.

'Chaka-chaka-chaka-chaka-chaka!'

The magpies descended on Mr Tucker.

'Flamin' fishfingers!' Mr Tucker rolled about. 'Now it's birds as well! They's making a nest!'

'That's not a bad idea,' Thug said, wriggling further in. 'It's all cosy.'

'And soft,' Slasher snuggled in too.

''Ere!' said Wally. 'There's bits of sardine in it!'

'I'm starving!' Pig grunted.

'Me too,' Gizzard agreed. 'I'm so hungry I could eat Wal's poo.'

The magpies started combing Mr Tucker's beard for tasty morsels.

'Stop it!' Jimmy shouted. 'Or we'll all be stuck.' He pecked viciously at the tangle, trying to free Biscuit.

Atticus wondered what to do. There were shreds of beard-jumper all over the deck.

SCWHIPP! SCHWIPP! SCHWIPP!

PECK! PECK! PECK!

It wouldn't be long before Biscuit and Jimmy cut themselves free.

Just then, the cabin door banged open. Michael charged up the steps. 'The Crown Jewels are safe,' he panted. 'And we found this.' Michael was clutching a green bottle marked SLEEPING POTION. 'Callie and Mum are looking for the hairpins, Atticus,' he yelled. 'So you can zap Biscuit.'

Atticus felt his fur fluff. His good ear twitched. So did his chewed one. He didn't need hairpins.

POP. POP. POP. POP. He pinged out the claws on one forepaw and beckoned.

Michael looked at him, puzzled. Then he understood. 'Great idea, Atticus!' He held the bottle out to Atticus, keeping his hand steady. 'Be careful you don't get it on your paw though.'

Atticus dipped his claws into the sleeping potion.

Ginger Biscuit and the magpies watched in horror.

'NO!' Ginger Biscuit slashed furiously at the beard-jumper. 'Hurry up, you useless birdbrains, he's going to claw us to sleep.'

'Got it in one.' Atticus advanced and stretched out his paw.

'Chaka-chaka-chaka-chaka-chaka!' The magpies flapped and tangled.

'Let's start with you guys,' Atticus said.

PRICK! 'Zzzzzz.' Pig was asleep.

PRICK! 'Zzzzzz.' Gizzard dozed off.

PRICK! 'Snnnnooooorrrrr.' Wally was under.

PRICK! 'Chakzzzzchakzzzz!' Slasher conked out.

PRICK! 'It's like *Sleeping Beauty*!' Thug sighed, closing his eyes.

Atticus dipped his claws again. 'Your turn.'

PRICK! 'I'll get you for this, Claw!' Jimmy Magpie stopped flapping. His eyelids closed.

'Night-night, Biscuit!' PRICK! PRICK! PRICK! PRICK! Atticus sank four claws into Biscuit's beefy backside, just to be on the safe side.

'MMYYYAAAWWWWwwwwwnnnnnnnnnnn.' Ginger Biscuit went out like a light.

'Good work, Atticus!' Mr Tucker struggled to his foot. He produced a pair of scissors from somewhere in his trousers.

SNIP! SNIP! SNIP! The rest of the beard-jumper, full of magpies and a ginger cat tumbled to the deck.

'I's been growing that since I was a baby!' Mr Tucker shook his head sadly at his fallen fleece. 'Oh well, I'll have to ask Edna if she can knit me a new one.'

Edna! Atticus turned in horror. They had forgotten all about Mrs Tucker.

Just then Mrs Tucker struggled towards them in her thick rubber trousers. 'Where were you?' She bashed Mr Tucker on the head with her last sardine. 'I held Klob off for as long as I could. Thanks to you, she got away again!'

'Not now, Edna!' Mr Tucker fell over again. 'Someone pass me me leg!' he pleaded.

WHIP!

Atticus didn't see the fishing line until it was too late.

Everyone looked up in horror. The remains of Mr Tucker's beard-jumper were being winched into the air with Ginger Biscuit and the magpies still tangled up in it, snoring loudly.

'Hahahahahahah!' from somewhere nearby Zenia Klob let out a hideous cackle. 'You didn't know I was the seven-times Siberian pike-fishing champion, did you, Velk?'

'Klob's got me tackle!' Mr Tucker yelled. 'Do something!'

The beard-jumper swung dangerously above them for a few seconds, then landed on *The Jolly Jellyfish*.

PUTTPUTTPUTTPUTTPUTTPUTT.

'Bye-bye! Suckers!' Klob shouted.

'And me boat!' Mr Tucker cried in anguish. 'She must have untied the ropes when we wasn't looking!'

Atticus knew he was right. The barge was drifting. Klob was getting away! With Ginger Biscuit and the magpies! After everything he'd done! He leapt on to the railing, ready to launch himself into the Thames. He'd swim after *The Jolly Jellyfish* if he had to.

'No, Atticus.' Mrs Tucker squashed him smartly with her rubber hat. 'You've done all you can. You've saved the Crown Jewels and the monarchy. I'd say that was enough for one day.'

'Edna's right.' Mr Tucker sniffed. 'Anyway,' he managed a smile, 'she's nearly out of shaarrrk faaarrrtt. They won't get faaarrrr.'

Callie scooped Atticus up. 'You're staying with us,' she said, burying her face in his fur.

'You're definitely not going anywhere.' Michael tickled him under the chin.

'Except home,' Mrs Cheddar agreed.

Home. Atticus purred throatily. It sounded good to him. He realised he was especially looking forward to telling Mimi his adventures and having a nice walk on the beach at sunset.

At the airport, Inspector Cheddar paced to and fro in front of the check-in desk.

His walkie-talkie crackled. It was HQ.

'Any sign of Klob?' The Police Commissioner demanded.

'Not yet, sir,' Inspector Cheddar replied.

'Remember, Cheddar,' the Commissioner warned, 'if she gives Agent Whelk the slip, it's up to you to catch her before she gets on that plane.'

'I understand, sir. She won't get away this time.'

'Good. I'll be there as soon as I can.' The walkie-talkie went silent.

At that moment, an elderly lady in a long rain-coat and woolly hat hobbled into the airport. Inspector Cheddar recognised her at once. *The*

Commissioner's mother! She looked exactly like she had in Toffany's, except as well as the fox fur she wore a mangy old black-and-white feather boa around her neck. Inspector Cheddar grimaced. It still had the beaks on.

'Mother Commissioner!' he squeaked. 'I'm so sorry about what happened the other day.'

The elderly lady glared at him. 'So you should be,' she said. She looked about. 'Vere's my son? He told me to meet him here so I can see him arrest Klob and get another medal.'

'He's on his way,' Inspector Cheddar said. 'Shouldn't be long.'

The old lady groaned. 'My corns are killing me,' she complained. 'I vant to sit down.'

'Why don't you go through to the departure lounge and have a seat there,' Inspector Cheddar suggested. 'It might be safer.'

'For sure, if you insist.'

Phew! Inspector Cheddar watched the elderly lady make her way through the unmanned security gate. He didn't want to risk the Commissioner's mother getting hairpinned by Klob!

As soon as she disappeared from view he heard

a wild cackle and the sound of running feet. He frowned. *Maybe her corns had got better after all?*

NEE-NAW! NEE-NAW! NEE-NAW!

The Commissioner raced into the building. 'I've just heard! Klob's given Whelk the slip again. She's on her way here with Biscuit and the magpies.'

'What about my family?' Inspector Cheddar gasped. 'Are they all right?'

'All safe,' the Commissioner grunted. 'Including Atticus.'

Inspector Cheddar breathed a sigh of relief. 'Don't worry, sir,' he said. 'I've got everything covered. When Klob shows up, I'll nab her.' He paused. 'By the way, I sent your mother through to the departure lounge.' He swallowed, trying to think of something nice to say. 'She looked lovely in that new feather boa.'

'What are you talking about, Cheddar?' The Commissioner barked. 'My mother's playing bridge with Her Majesty. And she doesn't have a feather boa.'

'But . . .' Inspector Cheddar went white.

VVRRROOOOOOMMMMMMMM!

'Was that an aeroplane taking off?' The

Commissioner's eyes were popping. 'Hang on a minute. My mother, did you say? You didn't think . . .' His face went purple. 'YOU IDIOT!'

Inspector Cheddar sighed. *Traffic cones again.* Oh well, he thought. Who cares? At least my family is safe.

25

Buckingham Palace
London

Atticus Grammaticus
Cattypuss Claw Esq.
2 Blossom Crescent
Littleton-on-Sea

Dear Atticus,

I am writing to thank you for doing
such a wonderful job of saving the
monarchy and stopping Zenia Klob and
her gang from stealing the Crown
Jewels. If it hadn't been for your
bravery, Philip and I would be living
in a B&B in Scotland and tourists

would have nothing to look at. (Not
that there's anything wrong with B&Bs,
of course. To tell you the truth I
quite fancy the idea but Philip likes
a choice of at least six bedrooms to
sleep in, which could be expensive.)
Anyway, as I was saying, we think you
did a great job and you thoroughly
deserve your promotion to Police Cat
Sergeant.

You'll be pleased to know that I have
granted Inspector Cheddar a Royal
Pardon for allowing Zenia Klob, Ginger
Biscuit and those miserable magpies
to escape to Siberia. Apparently Klob
cunningly disguised herself as the
Police Commissioner's mother, Biscuit
pretended to be a fox fur and the
magpies were roped together as a beaky
feather boa. I've told the Commissioner
not to make such a fuss about it.
Honestly, anyone could have made the
same mistake! Besides, who wants them

here? I'd rather they were in Siberia
than cluttering up my prisons.

One last thing. I have written to Agent
Whelk and her husband Herman Tucker
to commend them for their bravery and
to wish him well with growing his new
beard-jumper. I was so pleased to
hear that *The Jolly Jellyfish* washed
up undamaged in Kent. I must say that
shark fart seems a remarkably efficient
fuel. Philip and I are considering
switching to it to help save the
environment.

So, congratulations on a job well done,
Atticus. I do hope our paths will cross
again in the future, and that you will
find the time to come and teach the
corgis some manners!

Best wishes,
Elizabeth
(Still your queen thanks to AGCC)

Atticus finished reading the letter aloud to Mimi. They were sitting by the beach hut in Littleton-on-Sea where they usually met. Atticus's tummy was full. Mrs Tucker had wrapped a couple of sardines in a new red handkerchief (embroidered with his full name in tiny white writing just like the one Ginger Biscuit had shredded) so that they could have a picnic together. Atticus sighed happily. It was great to be home.

Mimi squeezed his paw. 'I'm really proud of you,' she said. She tied the handkerchief in a knot round his neck. 'And I love your new police-cat badge.'

'Inspector Cheddar had it made specially,' Atticus said. He lowered his chin and peered down. The new police-cat badge was pinned to the handkerchief. He couldn't really see what it said but it twinkled at him in the sunlight.

'You deserve it,' Mimi said. She stepped away from him and started preening her whiskers. Suddenly she smiled. 'I missed you, you know.'

'Did you?' Atticus's heart leapt.

'Yes.' The smile turned into a frown. 'But I was quite cross with you too.'

'Oh,' he said, feeling dejected.

'While you were out having all the fun saving ravens, I was stuck here doing nothing,' Mimi complained. 'Next time you have an adventure, Atticus Grammaticus Cattypuss Claw, I want to be part of it. Okay?'

'Okay,' Atticus agreed. 'But don't get mad if I have to dye you a different colour.'

'I won't,' Mimi promised.

Atticus got up. He yawned and stretched. If he was going to have another adventure he needed to get fit. Not fit like Ginger Biscuit, in a weird cat weight-lifting sort of way, but a bit thinner, like he had been when he first arrived in Littleton-on-Sea as the world's greatest cat burglar. 'Would you like to go for a walk?' he asked.

'I'd love to,' Mimi said.

'Town or beach?'

'Definitely beach.'

'I hoped you'd say that,' Atticus said. 'I want to

watch the sunset.'

'Me too.'

'Let's go then.'

Purring softly, the two cats strolled along the sand until the sun set in a red stripy sky and everything was black and brown, like Atticus.

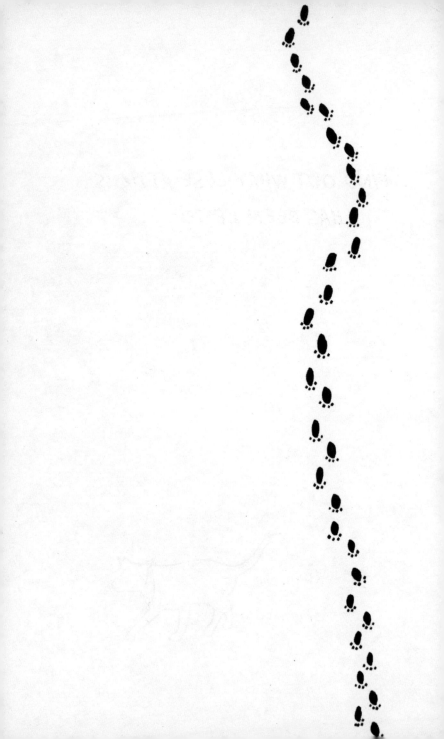

FIND OUT WHAT ELSE ATTICUS
HAS BEEN UP TO . . .

OUT NOW!

JENNIFER GRAY

ATTICUS CLAW

CLAW

Breaks the Law

'Atticus puts the
WOW! into meow!'
Jeremy Strong

ff

COMING IN
AUGUST 2013!

JENNIFER GRAY

ATTICUS CLAW

CLAW

Lends a Paw

'Atticus puts the WOW! into
meow!' Jeremy Strong